BETWEEN TWO WORLDS

BETWEEN TWO WORLDS

Cheyenne van Langevelde

To Rosemary Sutcliff, for revealing to me, now many years ago, the ancient beauty of the Celts and the Romans, and who, by her literary talents, developed a passion in me for their culture and history.

And to my Lord and Savior, Jesus Christ, Who gives us all a hope and a future.

TABLE OF CONTENTS

AUTHOR'S NOTE

This book began, in all honesty, with a dream.

Not any sort of grand vision or inner voice that demanded this story be written or that it was worth all the gold in the world. Not anything great like that. More like the sort of odd, vivid scenes that cross your mind when deeply asleep, that later you wake up and wonder how they ever managed to pop into your head.

I remember texting my friend, Bekkie, about it the next morning, saying how funny I thought it was, coming out of nowhere. She replied that yes, it was interesting, but more so, that I needed to turn it into a story. So I suppose that this book really owes its existence to her.

At the time, I had laughed and said something along the lines of, "Sure, one of these days when I've run out of other ideas to write." A few months later, when everyone was announcing their NaNoWriMo projects and encouraging me to give it a go, I succumbed and, hardly realizing what I was doing, began planning out *Between Two Worlds*. So with thousands of writers around the world during the month of November, I was typing furiously.

27 days. 52,173 words. And the first draft was done. It took months of editing to make the novel what it is now, but the heart of the story remains the same.

I have tried my best to present an accurate picture of Roman life during the first century A.D., including the treatment of slaves and the persecution of the early Christian martyrs. That said, there are some details that I have chosen to take liberties with.

For instance, while history says that both of Boudicca's daughters were raped and then murdered, I have kept one of her daughters alive for some years longer. Furthermore, there are no dates for the deaths of Aquila and Priscilla, only that they were martyred during the first century.

As the Bible was compiled into one volume much later in history, I have only the letter to the Romans as Scripture in here. Herodotus' *Histories* is also mentioned, though there is little evidence that they were widely read by women. Although many women were scholars in their own right, they were few and far between; people like Julia and Enid were not the norm.

At the time when I was writing this book, I didn't have any grand schemes for it. I even said that I was surprised how much I ended up being proud of the thing. For me, it was just "a fun story" in a time period that I personally enjoyed reading about. It wasn't until later that I realized it was so much more than that.

Closing up the fifth round of edits in preparation for querying, I was reading over the last few lines of the book. I had been working hard on it for months and felt completely one with the story; then, reading the very last line, I was so oddly disconnected I ended up staring at the wall for several minutes, trying to understand what was going on. I hadn't realized that through Enid and through her story, I was, in many ways, telling my own. Many of the events in my own life inspired happenings in hers—albeit not exactly the same. And because of this, there was no difference between her character and my own; they had felt one and the same until that moment.

It was then that I finally understood that *Between Two Worlds* is more than just an interesting story. At its heart, it is a quest for identity in the midst of loss and pain. I hadn't realized until then how much of Enid's struggles and searching was a mirror of my own.

This story, though polished from its first draft state, is still raw. There are some things that cannot be smoothed over by editing; history is too stark a contrast against what we often romanticize it to be. But I do hope that you enjoy it, even if just as entertainment, if not more. And I hope, for Enid and Lucius' sake, that I've done them and their story justice.

So, if you are willing, let's travel back some centuries to Roman-occupied Britannia...

PROLOGUE

IT BEGAN WITH a whisper.

A mere snatch of conversation heard while on his way to the baths; and yet in that half-breath of a moment, the snippet of song on Justus' lips was replaced with choking silence.

He minded then how sharply the damp, mossy walls of the fort stood out against the pale grey of sky; how loud the tramp of the guards sounded as they strolled back and forth above the gates. A cough from an auxiliary on the battlements above him thundered in his ears. The world darkened to his senses and then grew vivid once more.

Stumbling back to his barracks, all thoughts of a bath forgotten, Justus paused before the door of the squat building, identical to the legionaries' quarters of every army camp across the Roman Empire. Looking back, he gazed at the town and the green, rolling landscape that sloped away from the *castrum* the hillfort was built upon. A cold breath of wind stirred the scraggly bushes leaning against the walls, an empty, mocking rustling. The clouds above parted for an instant, revealing brilliant azure beyond the bleak gloom; and then it was gone. Gone like the fleeting joy of the past year.

His throat constricted and he turned away, stepping into the damp darkness of the barracks.

Within seconds, his eyes adjusted to the dusty gloom and he made his way to his humble centurion's cot, settling down upon it. Faint creaks and scuffles could be heard from his soldiers as they moved about, discarding their embossed-leather armor for woolen tunics and tight-fitting breeks beneath. The air reeked of musty straw, leather, sour metal, and sweat. A couple auxiliaries passed him on their way out to the baths, but neither of them said a word.

Justus placed his head in his hands, his mind whirling with what he had overheard.

Quintus says we shall be marching out soon. That British whore is gathering forces for a rebellion; her hosts have already besieged Camulodunum. We are to send a large vexillatio *to hold back the tide while we wait for reinforcements....*

Justus lifted his head, helplessness overwhelming him. Within a matter of days, he would be required to fight against a people that were not his own by birth, but among whom he had strong ties—ties not easily broken.

He leaned back against the cold stone and closed his eyes, fragments of the past year flooding his mind....

Water dripping endlessly.

Dampness enshrouding the intermittently-spaced torches.

A foggy glare glistening off wet stone walls.

Muffled cries.

A strange sense of excitement, the like of which he had never felt before—and yet a feeling of horrible dread.

'What be our mission this time?' Justus had asked as he marched swiftly through the dungeons of the fort.

'Boudicca hath been imprisoned,' came the swift reply from the battle-scarred centurion beside him.

'Boudicca—the wife of Prasutagus, king of the Iceni?'

'Aye, the same.'

'What means her presence here, then?' Justus turned his body sideways to squeeze through a doorway.

The other man shrugged. 'I know not. 'Tis none of my concern. We'—he paused to grab the ring of keys on his belt—'have more important business.'

'Like what?'

'Like what?' The man threw his head back and laughed. 'What dost thou think? Her daughters are here. General Aquinas wants them murdered—but he did not forbid us to have some fun first.'

Justus stared for a moment before he understood. A burning wave of shame swept over him and he laughed awkwardly. He knew not how else to respond without being ridiculed.

As they entered the cell, the centurion turned to him. 'Well, which one dost thou prefer?'

Justus blinked in the gloom. Two girls, one no more than a child, stared at them, terror in their eyes. 'The older one.' The words were out of his mouth before he realized it.

His companion grunted and stepped forward, taking up the little girl and swinging her over his shoulder. Her frightened screams tore through the air as he carried her off, but he paid no mind.

Justus gawked at the girl in front of him, his ears still ringing with her sister's shrieks. This was wrong.

His mouth was dry, and he was none too confident with the Celtic tongue, but he doubted the girl could understand Latin. 'Dewch yma,' he said softly.

She stared back, a whimper escaping her lips.

Justus ran his fingers through his hair in frustration and switched to his mother tongue. 'I want to help thee.'

The girl only blinked in confusion.

Taking the time to explain himself would be useless. If he did not leave soon, someone else would come to claim her.

Stepping forward, he tore a strip from his tunic and tied it over her mouth to muffle her screams. Then he threw his cloak around her and swung her over his shoulder, leaving the filthy cell.

Once out of the dungeons, he made his way to the back entrance of the fort. When the sentry's back was turned, he slipped through the small postern gate. Then he broke into a run, slinking through the deserted streets and never stopping until he reached the fields beyond the town, where he set down his burden and undid the gag around her mouth.

Now in the light, he could see the pale beauty that had been obscured by prison gloom. Tawny braids fell to her waist, and the white sun glistened in her green-gold eyes, which shimmered like glowing bronze. A crystal tear slipped down her freckled face. She clenched her hands at her sides, fear and anger burning in her glance.

'Do not be afraid; I will not hurt thee.' He shook his head, remembering. 'Thou dost not understand what I say.'

'I know the tongue,' came the soft, halting reply. Her voice was like a stream over stones, smooth and icy cold. 'Why wouldst thou rescue me?'

'Because—I…. Because to do any less would be wrong.'

'What is thy name?'

He blinked. 'Justus Julius Septimius. And thine?'

'Brenyn.'

He hesitated before speaking again. They were far from Iceni lands, and the Romans would certainly come after her if they discovered that she was still alive.

'Brenyn, thou must come with me,' Justus said urgently, holding out his hand.

She took it, her hand small and fragile in his large, calloused one. 'Where wilt thou take me?'

'To a British hunting companion of thine own tribe. I am certain he will keep thee safe until thou canst return home. Now come….'

Justus opened his eyes. How simple everything had seemed then—simple, and yet not so. His mother had raised him to know what was right, what was courteous, but even now he sometimes wondered if the consequences were worth what he had done.

Gazing into Brenyn's green-gold eyes in the weeks that followed the escape, Justus knew that he could never love another as he did her. Though Roman soldiers could not legally marry under Roman law, many of them had common-law wives. And so Justus wedded Brenyn according to the laws of her people, and she bore him a son.

He had kept all of this hidden from his fellow legionaries for a year now, especially from his uncle, who was known for his hatred of the British. With war on the horizon, if someone found out that he was wed to Boudicca's daughter, Justus would be considered guilty of treason. But he had to warn Brenyn of what was coming. He had sworn to protect both her and their child, and not even his loyalty to Rome could come before that oath.

He rose from his cot and crossed the ground between his barracks and the legate's lodging. As head of the legion, the legate was permitted a larger and better living space than his officers, yet the dim room was lit only by a small window in the outside wall and an oil lamp on the legate's table.

Justus raised his hand in a stiff salute. '*Ave*, Quintus.'

The young legate raised his head. '*Ave*, Justus. What brings thee here?'

'I wish to beg leave for a few hours.'

Quintus' cold, dark eyes looked him over for several seconds. 'Where wilt thou go?'

'Since when does the legate require such information?' Justus took pains to speak respectfully, but he could not help the undertone of urgency which crept into his voice.

'Since I received news of the Trinovantes' uprising. I cannot suffer news of our march upon them to be made known. And I know that thou hast many friends among the Britons.'

'If I swear by Mithras that I will breathe no word of our counter-attack at Camulodunum, wilt thou let me go?'

Several tense moments passed. Cold sweat trickled down Justus' back, but he looked Quintus steadily in the eye.

At last, the legate straightened and clasped his hands on the table before him. 'I know thee to be a man who abides by thy word. If thou wilt swear by Mithras, I will permit it. But thou must be back before curfew.'

'I swear by Mithras that I will speak nothing concerning our plans for attack, to Briton or Roman.'

'Very well.' The legate returned his attention to the parchment before him, signaling with his hand for Justus to depart.

Justus saluted once more and then left, marching with long strides to the gate and the town beyond.

'Halt! What be the password?' the guard shouted from atop the gate, shattering the peaceful evening silence.

Justus checked at the sentry's loud voice, hesitating a moment as his mind raced to remember the two words that would allow him entry beyond the garrison's walls.

'*Caligo sanguis.*' Blood mist.

Justus was struck with the irony of it all, but did not have time to dwell on it. A moment later, the gates opened and the young centurion passed through, walking purposefully through the cluttered streets of Durovernum Cantiacorum.

Away from the marketplace, the Roman buildings disappeared. Only the round, earthen huts of the Britons remained, scattered here and there with smoke rising lazily from their thatched roofs. As in all things, it seemed, the British peoples remained resilient against Roman rule, quietly living as if the Roman invasion had never taken place. Justus wondered how many of these Celts would join up against his cohort when they learned of the coming attack.

Within a few minutes, he reached the bothy on the outskirts of the town and knocked firmly on the door. The tiny street was deserted at this hour of the day, since most were supping the evening meal.

The door opened to reveal the pale features of his friend Halwyn. 'Justus. What bringeth thee here at this time?'

'I cannot discuss it out in the open.'

Halwyn nodded and opened the door wider.

Justus slipped inside and blinked as darkness descended. Yellow light from the center hearth spilled onto the floor, illuminating the simple interior. In one corner was a loom, and in another lay straw pallets stacked upon each other. Halwyn's wife was bent over the fire, stirring something that bubbled and filled the air with a mouth-watering smell. Yet Justus' gaze merely brushed over these things, seeking for the shadow that arose at his entrance and came towards him.

He embraced Brenyn tightly, feeling her slender form tremble slightly as she breathed. Releasing her, he spoke softly in the Celtic tongue. 'Brenyn, I need to speak with thee.'

'Speak. I am listening.'

Glancing at Halwyn and his wife, who attempted to give them privacy, Justus motioned for Brenyn to sit back down in the corner. He inhaled deeply before speaking, feeling ever more strongly the desperation of the situation. 'Hast thou received recent news from thy mother?'

Brenyn's gaze flickered up and met his. 'If thou speakest of the rebellion, I have indeed received news of it. But my mother has not sent word to me since I wrote to her of my safe presence in Durovernum Cantiacorum.' She hesitated in speaking the long Roman name.

'Brenyn.' He took her cold, slender hands and held them gently. 'My legion, as much of us as are stationed here, must fight thy people a few days hence to liberate the town they have captured.'

Anger flashed in her eyes. 'My people are only taking revenge for what they have lost. Surely thee, of all the Romans, would best understand why they do this.' Her next words were forced out between clenched teeth. 'Thy people raped and murdered my sister before my mother's eyes, treated my mother shamefully, and whipped her besides. They stole our lands and enslaved my people…' Her voice softened. 'Thou wert not like them and for that I forgave thee. Thou lovest me, and I thee. But it changes not what they have done.'

'I know.' Justus pursed his lips in silence. 'Should I fight alongside my men, I would be slaying thy kind. And should I keep loyalty to thy tribe, I would be accounted a traitor to my own…I am caught between two worlds. There is no place for me in this, and yet I have no choice. I cannot shirk my duty. Cowardice is looked on kindly by neither thy people nor mine.'

The anger was gone from her eyes now, and only a bitter pain remained in its stead—the same pain that throbbed in his own chest and caught in his throat.

'I understand,' she said.

He gazed into her eyes and tried to memorize every detail of her fair face, knowing he might never see her again. 'I fear for thee. Wrathful men do not see reason, and they will slay all in their path.'

'Where will I go? There is no place for me, just as there is none for thee.'

Neither of them spoke for a time, Brenyn waiting for an answer, and Justus knowing there was none to give.

'I will do what I can,' he said at last. 'I must go; I have to return before curfew. I shall attempt to send word before we march.' He rose to his feet.

Halwyn and his wife glanced up from their stew as he rose, then returned to their food, still attempting to give Justus and Brenyn an appearance of privacy.

The babe in the cradle at his feet whimpered, and Brenyn bent to pick him up. 'Say farewell to thy son before thou goest.'

Something within Justus broke and he swallowed hard. He took the child in his arms, feeling the vividness of living warmth envelop him. He stared into his son's large, dark eyes and the child blinked, another mewl escaping his tiny mouth. Black, silky feathers of hair brushed against Justus' arm, soft against his skin. He bent and kissed his son's forehead before returning him to his mother, regret staining this bittersweet farewell.

Justus watched his wife as she placed the babe back in his cradle, feeling he had no right to ask affection of her, since soon he would be forced to slay her kinsmen.

She knew this and yet did not shrink away. Locking her arms around his neck, she breathed into his ear, 'When I wed thee, I knew, as perhaps thou didst not, what this might cost me. Now our love must be tested. May it hold strong in the face of bloodshed and cruel loss.'

Words failed him and he did not speak for some time. 'If anything happens and I perish on the battlefield, go to my uncle. Tell him Lucius is his grandnephew. I will send him word by my own hand.' Then he bent and kissed her farewell.

PART I

I stand between two worlds
There is no middle ground for me
The tears that fall
Have wanted it all
There is no return for me
One look is all it took and I fall apart

Chapter I

T HE YEAR DAWNED *grey and frosted and bitterly cold.*

It was the year of our Lord 78, by the Roman calendar 831: the ninth year of the reign of Roman Emperor Titus Flavius Vespansianus, known to his people as Vespasian; the year of the consulship of Novius and Commodus; the year that the unstoppable legions of the Roman Empire conquered the Ordovice and Silure tribes of Britannia; and the year that Gnaeus Julius Agricola replaced Sextus Julius Frontinus as the governor of Roman Britain. But all that meant little to me.

I am—I was—Enid, daughter of Ioan, the chieftain of our clan, lord of three valleys and the forest surrounding them, whose warriors numbered in the hundreds, and of many bondservants and freedmen. And on the turning of the year, as the eastern sky paled to silvery pearl and the white sun shone gloomily from the wintry heavens, the Roman Empire was only a dream, a far-off sigh of something beyond my understanding—occasionally spoken of by the clan elders, but nothing more. The valley and the mountains were my world—the river and the forest, the sky and the wind. Our people were our own and we cared little for the great kingdoms beyond our lands that posed no threat to us.

Yet could I have foreseen that when the snows melted away I would no longer be in the place I loved best, it is in my heart that perhaps I would have been different. I would have smiled more at the humourous pretensions of my younger sisters and lingered longer as I kissed the youngest. I would have laughed at the jests of my brothers, been more willing to serve alongside my mother, encouraged and appreciated my father—but all that matters little now.

The waters of Lethe offer only one passage, and woe to the soul that wishes to return through.

For we can never go back....

The first day of spring began as any other, that fateful year. I rose early to bring water from the stream that ran beyond the outskirts of the village. Coming back, as the sun began to peep its rosy face over a sleeping world, I passed Telyn on his way for a morning hunt.

Telyn was the hunting companion of my brothers, with hair the colour of a night sky without stars, shining grey eyes, and a winsome smile. I was not the only maiden to lose my heart to him, but I was the only one who received any attention from him, even if for most of my childhood he paid me only common courtesies.

He raised his hand in recognition. 'Enid, thou hast risen early this morn.' His words became small white clouds in the morning chill. He stopped walking when he reached my side, towering a good handbreadth above me.

I smiled, my cheeks burning at the pleasure of speaking to him alone. I thrust aside a loose strand of red hair that had fallen in front of my eyes. 'I could not sleep.'

Telyn shrugged, a dimpled smile sweetening his otherwise serious face. 'Fair enough. Was thy sleep troubled?'

'Nay, not at all. I slept well.'

'Good. There is no reason thou shouldst not.' He readjusted the strung bow on his shoulder. His other hand strayed out of habit to gently finger the fletching of the arrows in the quiver at his waist. The pale morning light shadowed his high cheek-bones, giving him a more thoughtful appearance than usual.

I swallowed and glanced away shyly, not knowing what else to say. Telyn himself gazed at the rays of sunshine piercing through the trees and lighting on the thatched roofs of the living places. I looked as well, the sight no less dear to me because of its familiarity.

Our village lay spread out in a wooded valley with the usual scattering of round huts that housed a family each, the animal pens close by, and the fields an hour's walk away.

Peat smoke rose thicker from the bothies, and I knew I should return home. I longed to linger with Telyn in the early dawn, but it would be unseemly—especially as a chieftain's daughter—to be seen alone with a youth at this early hour, however innocent our intentions might be.

'I wish thee a good hunting, Telyn.' My gaze flickered shyly to meet his.

'I thank thee, Enid.' He grinned and strode off, firm and steady, and I strengthened my grip on the water jar in my hands.

I treasured that rare moment in my memory. It was mine, and no one could take it from me.

At odd moments throughout the rest of the morning, a smile crossed my face at the memory, but if my mother noticed, she said nothing. It was often in my mind to wonder who would be my betrothed when the time came for me to be wedded. My father would choose, most likely to strengthen ties with a neighbouring clan. Our tribe was small, scarcely significant in the whole accounting of the Iceni people, but our harvests were plentiful, our woods were full of game, our men waxed strong, and we were left alone by the Redcrests from the empire over the sea. My father often said it was better to remain forgotten than to be constantly under threat of attack; yet an alliance by marriage would be to our benefit.

I would have no say in the matter, and could only hope that it would at least be someone I knew. It was too much to ask of the gods, whether Celtic or Roman, for Telyn to be my future husband. Yet still I dreamt of it—as did, I imagine, every other maiden in the village.

'Enid!'

My mother's voice dragged me out of my daydreams and I glanced up from the weaving lying idle in my hands.

'Enid, I wish for thee to summon thy brothers home for the meal. Thy father will not be back from his journey until evening.'

With a nod, I stood and stepped out of our hut into the sunlight.

The warmth of spring was slight, but after the icy darkness of winter it was much welcomed. The sun shone through the bare branches of the trees and smoke rose idly from the holes in the thatched roofs of the earthen huts, drifting to the clear sky above. And though the air still retained its chill, the slight breeze whispering among the ash and oak at the village's edge hinted at warmer days to come.

I passed many acquaintances on my way to the practice ring where I supposed my brothers to be, but I did not stop to speak to any of them beyond a casual greeting.

I recognized two of my brothers and called into the sea of faces of those that charged and ran towards each other in mock combat. 'Ffionn! Ilar!' I had to repeat their names, which were lost among the tumult, but at last the pair turned and came to me, their clothes darkened with sweat.

Ffionn was the first to speak. 'Aye, Enid?' His face, usually a reddish hue, was scarlet from the exercise. He was the eldest and tallest of all my brothers and still claimed the place of strongest, though Ilar often beat him in matches.

'Mother sent me to fetch thee both for the midday meal,' I replied. A smile spread across my face, one of pride, for I knew they were some of the best warriors in our village.

Ilar, much shorter but the more solidly built of the two, wiped sweat from his brow. 'We will come.'

I nodded in farewell and made my way to the chieftain's hall in search of the harper, Caradoc. My youngest brother, Brynmor, would undoubtedly be with him.

A peaceful, drowsy stillness lay over the great chieftain's hall. I paused for several moments as my eyes adjusted to the gloom. The hall was built much like our wattle-and-daub huts, but it was large enough to hold all the village at any given time. Little could be seen in the shadows that lay beyond reach of the sunlight spilling through the doorway. The door and the hole in the roof above lent scarcely any light, and there were no torches lit at this hour, but a small fire burned on the central raised hearth.

A ripple of notes echoed softly amid the murmur of voices in the hall, the harpist and his pupil oblivious to my presence. I walked towards them and sat down on the rushes-strewn floor. A harpist was always held in high honor so I waited respectfully for them to finish and kept my hands folded in my lap. I understood little of what they said, for the art of harping was a mystery to me.

At last, Caradoc finished and looked up at me, smiling. 'Thy brother knows almost as much as I do of this instrument.' He gestured to the wooden harp in his hands. 'Perhaps soon he will take my place as bard to the chieftain.'

My brother smiled slightly, shaking his head. 'Nay, that I will never be.'

Caradoc laughed, a sweet, mellow sound. 'Thou art too modest. But come, methinks thy sister is come to fetch thee home to eat. Music is a beautiful thing, but 'tis not food.'

Brynmor rose to his feet, his nimble form barely perceptible in the firelit shadows, murmuring something under his breath; thanking his tutor, I supposed.

Once out in the sunlight, I asked Brynmor what he had said, but he showed no interest in conversation, his dark brows knit in concentration. Giving up, I held my peace. He retreated often into this strange silence, preferring to keep his thoughts to himself than to speak them aloud.

Ffionn and Ilar were not so. Over the midday meal, they recounted some happening in the ring to my sisters and me with such excitement that my mother hushed our noise. Ilar pinched his lips together and attacked his stew with a frown, but Ffionn winked at me. I choked back another laugh as he imitated the two brothers on either side of him, one thoughtful and brooding, the other irritated and silent.

A youth dashed through the open door and stopped before the table, panting from exertion. It was Telyn.

My heart skipped a beat as I instinctively dropped my eyes to my empty bowl. My ears burned both with delight at seeing him and embarrassment at being seated among the bairns of my family, even though I had seen thirteen summers. I wished him to think well of me and not consider me still a mere child.

But he did not seem to even notice me. 'Ffionn, Ilar, Brynmor, I would fain speak with thee.'

'Why? Didst stumble upon some faeries?' Ffionn jested.

I gazed at Telyn's face, marking how the firelight danced in his grey eyes, yearning for him to acknowledge me, but he did not.

''Tis no laughing matter,' Telyn replied, once he caught his breath. 'The Redcrests have built a new fort a few bow-shots from our valleys.'

'What? Since when?' Ilar snapped. He seemed ready to jump to his feet and slay all the Redcrests with his bare hands.

A half-forgotten memory surfaced in my mind—a legion marching north, blinding sunlight reflecting off gold armor, endless straight lines of warriors with glittering spears. A mysterious, forbidden fascination had embedded itself in my heart that day, and whenever the infrequent subject of Rome was brought up, I could not help but wonder about those strange people from over the sea.

What did it mean that the Redcrests had built a town so near our tribal grounds?

Telyn shrugged. 'I do not know. Perhaps during the winter months. I only saw the fort, buzzing with soldiers and towns-people, and all sorts coming and going from the gates. But they will find us soon, and then we will remain hidden no longer.'

'This news is best saved for the council, when Ioan returns,' my mother said softly, giving the youths a meaningful look and glancing at the young girls still spooning stew into their mouths.

I bit my cheek in frustration, longing to know what my father would say. I had no place in council meetings and would have to wait even longer than my brothers to learn the consequence of Telyn's tidings.

My father arrived that evening with the men of his bodyguard. After speaking briefly to my mother, he went straight to the council and did not return until far into the night.

I heard my brothers and my father come in, but they said little for fear of waking my sisters, who were snoring softly beside me. My father and mother talked long into the night after the others had fallen asleep, but I could not decipher their whispered words, and soon I too was slumbering.

In the morning, my father and brothers were gone before I was awake, helping the others prepare the fields for the spring planting. My mother would not speak to me of what had been said last night, but I soon found an excuse to escape the dimness of our bothy and venture out into the daylight. Bearing food for my father and brothers in a bundle upon my back, I set out upon the track that led up the hills from our valley to the next one, humming a simple tune in rhythm to my footsteps.

The day was warm in comparison with the chill of yesterday, and perspiration soon rolled down my brow as I struggled up the steep incline. Damp leaves from last year's autumn made the many rocks scattered on the hillside slippery, and often I had to clamber up using my hands as well as my feet, lest I lose my footing and fall.

'Hail and well met, Enid!' A familiar voice crying from above startled me and I nearly tottered headlong off the leaf-strewn stones. I heard someone scrambling down from the heights and a moment later, Telyn stood before me, offering a hand to help me up.

I murmured my thanks as we struggled to reach the top, feeling a quiet knot of pride that he was helping me, even though the way was not so difficult. A pleasant warmth shot through my veins from where his hand gripped mine. Were it not for the exertion of climbing the steep hill, I would have found it difficult to keep a smile off my face.

At the top of the ridge, he let go of my hand and we both paused, panting to catch our breath. I cast my gaze from my beloved home valley to the one with the fields beyond, staring against the sun. Naked forest and grassy moorlands stretched as far as the eye could see, chariot-ways and rivers snaking their meandering way across the landscape to the dim, hazy shadow where hills rose far in the distance and where, some said, was the sea. But Rome had not left even this untamed wilderness untouched; one of their straight roads was partly visible in the rolling sweep of the land, and I fancied that I could see people and horses walking on it.

'Thou shouldst be more careful.' Telyn broke the peaceful silence between us, looking at me with concern.

'Why? I know the way well enough.' While I was flattered that he cared for my well-being, I felt a twinge of annoyance. Did he not believe me old enough to go by myself? Did he indeed see me as still a bairn?

'Aye, that well may be, but there are Redcrests close by. Oft we can hear the din of their town while we work.'

'What was decided at the council last night?' I hoped he would tell me, and I hoped also to shift the subject away from myself.

'They spoke of many things, but we have not yet come to a decision; only that we must watch and wait. Perhaps we will remain unnoticed.'

His tone was less hopeful than his words. Something in the way his eyes darted towards the town—trepidation, almost—made me begin to doubt how safe my world really was.

'Dost thou hope so? That we will remain unnoticed?' My voice was a whisper in my own ears.

Telyn drew his arm across his forehead, wiping away the sweat. He shrugged, but he did not smile. "Tis not for me to say. Some have mentioned bringing the matter before the whole village ere long… Thy father and brothers will be waiting for thee down below, and 'twill not be kind of me to keep thee from them. Come.'

He offered his hand once more with a swift smile, as if to banish the gloomy subject of the Redcrests, and I took it gratefully, a warm thrill spreading throughout my being.

The threat of Rome did not seem so dark and fearful with Telyn by my side.

That evening, the entire village gathered in the chieftain's hall, their faces both illuminated and shadowed by the firelight. My father and the other elders were amassed in the center, the warriors around them, and the rest of us fanning out towards the walls and doorway. The wind whistling its way through the open doorway and down the hole in the roof blew the blue peat smoke every which way, stinging my eyes. But I blinked back the tears and listened hard to the heated discussion. It was rare that a matter arose of such importance that all the village must hear it.

'We shall not ride out and plunder the city of the Redcrests,' my father was saying. 'Too much has happened since Boudicca's rebellion, and our strength is no longer what it once was.'

One of the other leaders fingered the ends of his long moustache, the flame-shadows dancing in his eyes. 'Then what dost thou suggest?'

I leaned in closer, nearly resting my hand on Telyn's shoulder, trying to hear over the whispered conversation of the crowd and the crying of someone's bairn.

'Watch and wait,' my father replied. 'Perhaps they will leave us in peace, for surely they must see that we are too small to be a threat.'

Another voice rose, but I could not see the speaker. 'What of escaping north and joining the Picts?'

'And leave behind the lands that have belonged to us for more years than man can count?' It was my brother, Ilar, who argued now. 'Methinks the Picts will be none so welcoming either. They are distrustful of everyone, including their fellow Britons.'

Murmurs followed this statement. For a moment, I wished I was one of the warriors, young enough to defend my home without the ties of family or old age to hold me back, yet old enough to join the council freely. As it was, I had to content myself with whispering in Telyn's ear and straining to hear his soft responses.

'What shall we do?' The gentle voice of Caradoc the harper silenced the tumultuous sea of hushed voices. I hardly recognized him without his beloved harp in his hands.

'What can any of us do?' I asked Telyn, but he only shrugged.

'Watch and wait,' repeated my father. 'If they threaten us, then we will speak of journeying elsewhere to make our home.'

'Shall we not attack them?' It was Ceredig who spoke now, the last druid still alive in our tribe. His hair, white from age, glimmered oddly in the dim light. 'It has always been our custom in times past.'

'Aye, when we had more men and stronger ties with the other tribes of the Iceni. We cannot defeat them alone.' My father's voice sounded drained and weary. 'And we cannot gather strength of arms without being speedily repulsed by the Redcrests. It might have been possible in my father's day, but not now. Nay, we can but watch and wait, praying to the gods that the Redcrests will overlook us and leave us in peace.'

Once outside the chieftain's hall, under the dim light of the moon and stars, I muttered under my breath, 'Why must we always attack the Redcrests? Since when have they done us any harm?'

Telyn, still close at hand, turned to me, his usually passive face shocked and almost furious. 'Speak not of that which thou dost not know!'

I inched away from him, surprised at the outburst. The chill of the early spring evening bit through my dress and I shivered, but not only because of the cold.

His face softened and he touched my shoulder briefly. 'Forgive me, Enid, I—I did not mean to speak so harshly to thee. 'Tis only that I cannot comprehend thy fascination with the Redcrests.'

''Tis no fascination, only curiosity. I cannot understand why Father hates them so. They seem like gods, the way their armor shines when they march on the road beyond our hills. Truly a people so skilled deserves our admiration, not our fear and hatred.'

Telyn looked at me for several moments. When he answered at last, his eyes were dark and sad. 'Enid, thou knowest well the fate of Boudicca and her daughters. Wouldst thou have us grovel before a people that dishonors and destroys our kind? Wouldst thou have us surrender our freedom and all that is ours to a nation that seeks only to make us their bondservants? What dost thou not understand? Our ways and theirs are different; there can never be peace between us. We will never be free as long as one of those accursed Redcrests walks on Celtic land.'

I swallowed hard, terribly cold without my cloak. What could I say? He was right—he must be right—but that did not stifle my desire to know more about these strange people who were so hated and forbidden.

Telyn's face gentled. 'Oh, Enid, I did not mean to hurt thee. Come, I will walk thee home.' He slipped his arm across my shoulders, his living warmth dispelling the deathly chill that had crept into my bones. I felt safe and cared for, and the evening frigidity and the threat of the Romans no longer seemed so near. If I could have had my wish, he would never have left; but it was not to be so.

All too soon, we were before the door of my family's dwelling place, and while I knew I had best be inside its walls, a part of me longed to stay outside with Telyn.

'Good night,' I murmured softly, my fingers gripping the skirt of my dress and my eyes bent towards the ground.

'Good night, Enid.' There was a hint of laughter in his voice. 'Wilt thou meet me on the hill just this side of the fields on the morrow? I have something I wish to tell thee.'

My head shot up. Trying in vain to calm the sudden racing of my heart, I only smiled, grateful for the darkness that hid my blushing face. 'Aye, I will.'

I watched, no longer sad, as his tall form slipped away in the clear twilight.

Dawn could not come soon enough.

CHAPTER II

THE AFTERNOON SUN filtered through the budding branches of the aspens, silver shadows snaking over the carpet of last autumn's leaves. The cold, damp ground kissed my bare feet as I skipped out of our village, but I scarcely noticed.

As I wound my way up the last hillrise that lay between our valley and the fields, my curiosity only grew. What did Telyn wish to tell me so secretly? Most of my guesses involved some sort of passionate declaration, but I could only wait to discover what it was.

'Thou hast come early.' Telyn's voice sounded over my shoulder and I whirled to see him approaching, the neck of his tunic darkened with sweat from working in the fields.

I smiled awkwardly, unsure if he was jesting. 'At least I came.' I felt my response foolish. My heart was racing faster than a horse on open moorland and I could do nothing to calm it.

He smiled warmly as he reached my side. 'Aye.' Then he glanced around, as if to assure himself that we were alone.

'What didst thou wish to tell me?' I prompted, when he did not speak.

Telyn's face flushed. 'First, Enid, thou must promise not to speak of this to anyone. Nothing is certain yet, and should word of our meeting be known, it might prove harmful to our reputations, regardless of our innocence.'

'I promise,' I vowed solemnly, more curious than ever.

The corners of his mouth twitched upward in a smile. 'I know thou wouldst not tell, but I wished to be certain.' He paused before continuing, looking at the ground as if to avoid my gaze. 'My father has given me freedom to choose my own bride.'

My heart leapt into my throat and I clenched my hands, trying to calm the turmoil within me.

Telyn raised his dark head and smiled again, but the playful light in his eyes became something deeper. 'I have yet to ask thy father, but I wish to wed thee.'

My world came to a standstill, hearing nothing but my pounding heart. My mouth fell open. 'Truly?' I forced out at last, my ears burning at my lack of a swift response. The silence crescendoed into birdsong and windless rustling among the bracken, but I only cared about the dimpled smile on Telyn's face and the sunlight shining in his grey eyes.

'Aye, Enid, truly.' He placed his hands on my shoulders and I could hardly contain my excitement. I never knew such happiness would be possible for me. Of course, he would still have to ask my father for my hand, but the time for thinking about that would come later.

'I can scarce believe it,' I whispered, feeling as though my face would break from smiling.

He laughed, not in mockery, but from joy that we both shared.

The laughter died in his throat as he caught sight of something behind me. The colour drained from his face and his hand flew towards the sheathed dirk on his hip, his other arm drawing me protectively towards himself.

I spun around as Telyn's arm enveloped me, but the elation that had filled my heart only moments before vanished like mist beneath the sun, terror taking its place.

Four men stood before us, all dark-skinned and dressed in strange clothing, speaking to one another in a clipped language that sounded harsh in my ears. Within moments, Telyn and I were surrounded.

They had to be Roman slave traders, of whom I had heard spoken in hushed whispers when Dalwyn's child disappeared two harvests before. But why were they here now? And what did they want?

That last question hovered eerily in my mind, and I was too afraid to answer it.

'Enid.' Telyn's breath was hot against my face. 'When I give the signal, thou must run swifter than the deer. Go towards the fields and raise the alarm.'

'And thee?' My voice quivered in fear.

'Never mind about me. Now run!' His hold on me loosened as they advanced on him, leaving me free to escape their clutching hands and plunge down the hillside.

Though I was nimble and used to the terrain, my footing slipped in my haste. I slid midway down the steep hill before I grabbed hold of a young sapling, halting my descent. Glancing behind me, I saw Telyn fighting hard, his blade red in the sunlight. Only one slaver was visible, and I hoped the others had already fallen—though that seemed an impossible hope, for even Telyn could not defeat four men at once armed only with his dirk.

Swallowing hard, I regained my feet and set off again towards the fields, praying to any of the gods who might be listening to keep Telyn safe. There was little hope of either of us escaping the slave traders without aid.

But I was too late.

Strong arms wrapped around me, lifting me above the forest floor and carrying me off. I screamed and kicked my unseen captor, hoping someone would hear me, but he squeezed me until it hurt to breathe. Stars danced in the back of my vision and the world turned as dark as night. I heard Telyn's voice shout my name from somewhere above, but when I tried to catch sight of him, something hard hit the back of my head and I knew no more.

When I came to my senses, I noticed first a gentle rolling movement, a subtle rise and fall that made me queasy. I opened my eyes to darkness and struggled to regain my bearings. For a brief moment, I entertained the horrid thought that my captors had blinded me. The next instant, the memories of what had happened came flooding back like the rushing of the stream by our village when it was swollen by the spring rains.

I attempted to move my hands to my eyes only to discover they were tied, as were my feet. My eyes, too, were bound, and my mouth gagged. A scream rose in my throat, but it could not escape. I could not begin to fathom where I was, for even the sounds I heard were foreign to me—a rhythmic beating of a drum with corresponding splashes. Voices spoke in a strange tongue, the same harsh language that my captors had used.

A moment later, large, rough hands loosed my bonds, save those around my wrists and feet. I squinted against the dim light of a wooden space and found myself staring into the weather-beaten, dark-haired face of a man who proceeded to untie the ropes around my ankles.

'Where am I?' I asked once my gag was removed, realizing a moment too late that he probably could not understand me.

The man rose to his feet and shouted at someone. Another voice answered him from somewhere above and he left me, closing the door to the tiny room. Glancing around in panic, I realized that I was among several other persons dressed in British garb, most of them bedraggled and worn. All of us had our hands bound.

'What is happening?' I ventured, my voice trembling.

Only one of them raised their head—a young woman cradling a bairn. Her face was like a mask, dull and dejected, and in her lifeless eyes I saw hopelessness. 'We have been enslaved by the Redcrests and are bound on what they call a ship. They will take us to their capital city and sell us as bondservants.'

Horror filled my heart. A voice inside me screamed against reality. This had to be a nightmare or cruel joke. 'But why?'

She shrugged, her shoulders barely moving. 'Who can say? To the Romans, we are barbarians fit only for slavery. Thy only hope is that thou wilt drown before we reach their "Eternal City."' Her final words were spoken with such deep loathing that I spoke no more.

Her child began to cry, a pitiful wailing that aroused compassion from the others. A few of them looked at the mother with pity and sympathy in their eyes. The woman began to sing softly, but a voice from above commanded silence and the mournful melody ended as if cut through with a knife.

Tears filled my eyes at this cruelty and I turned my gaze away. Most slept; others stared with dazed eyes at nothing in particular. A wave of shock and desperation swept over me and I looked down into my lap, the queasiness welling up inside me. My stomach growled for food, but bile rose up in my mouth all the same and I struggled to keep it down.

I tipped my head back against a wooden pole that ran from floor to ceiling, gasping at the dull pain of the bruise on my head hitting the wood. I leaned back more gingerly the second time, closing my eyes as hopelessness overwhelmed me in depressingly dark waves.

Would this nightmare ever end?

'Enid!'

It was Telyn's dear voice, and for a moment I wondered if my captivity had truly been but a dream. I saw the familiar sun-dappled woods surrounding our valleys and sighed with sweet relief, turning my head to see Telyn walking towards me with a smile lighting his face.

'Telyn, why didst thou call?'

Much to my surprise, he took my hands in his and replied, 'Come, the celebration hath begun and I wish to dance with thee.' He set off for our village, my hand still in his, and I followed him, laughing.

Within moments, we reached the firelit circle where couples whirled and stepped in perfect time to the lively music of the flute and drum. Those not dancing clapped along with the rest, watching those in the center with eager interest.

Before I realized it, I was swept into the throng and soon was matching the footwork of the others as Telyn led me around the ring. I could not begin to guess how long that dance went on, for it seemed to go on forever and yet finish too soon.

Telyn walked out of the circle as another dance began and I followed him, trying to catch my breath. Still holding his hand, I moistened my parched throat with the sweet, fire-hearted mead.

He lifted the cup to his lips and swallowed, his eyes twinkling in merriment. 'Ah, that is much better,' he said with a satisfied sigh. Then, 'Shall we go again?'

I smiled in response and we rejoined the encircling ring, now moving at a slower tempo, the bittersweet melody echoing up to the sky and then down again. Amidst the dancing, I heard a strange thumping that was not from our drums, and oft I turned my head to search for the source of the sound.

I never could discover what it was, though it grew ever louder and louder, drowning out the music and laughter and the warmth of Telyn's hands holding mine....

Icy-cold water poured down upon me and my eyes flew open as I gasped in shock. The compartment was dark, yet I could still make out the shadowy shapes of men, women, and children huddled in the depths of the ship. Gone was the full moonlight, gone the leaping flames of celebration, gone the warmth and familiarity of home. In its place was cold darkness, abandonment, and loneliness.

Thunder crashed outside, and the ship's timbers creaked and groaned beneath the strain of being tossed about on the sea. Every surge of water that slammed onto its decks sank through the cracks in the wood, raining down on us below. The stench of sick and human filth was overwhelming—within moments, I could no longer keep the contents of my stomach where they belonged and they mingled with the other putrescence on the floor.

At that moment, I cared for little but the heaving of my insides that seemed to rise and fall with the motion of the ship. I wished to die. Any fascination I once had for the Roman kind had long since vanished, and I wondered that I had ever cared about them.

The words of the woman I had spoken to earlier came back to me and I whispered them amidst the crashing of the storm around me. *'Thy only hope is that thou wilt drown before we reach their Eternal City.'* I closed my eyes to better concentrate on something besides the nausea and the storm raging above my head.

Would life as a slave in Rome truly be so terrible that death was preferable? I had heard many times how the daughters of Boudicca had been treated at the hands of the Romans—were slaves handled any better? I knew little about these people beyond rumors that made their way into our valleys. What were they like?

More importantly, would I ever win my freedom? Would I ever see my family again? And Telyn—!

Tears trickled down my face as a wave of grief washed over me, stronger than those that threatened to wreck the ship.

Had Telyn managed to escape from the slavers unharmed? Had the village sent out a search party for me, or had they given me up as lost? I did not think Telyn would easily abandon me after his declaration of love, but here in the midst of the darkness and the storm, I could almost believe I was forgotten. Was there any hope of ever seeing the people I loved again?

My broken heart cried out in silent anguish, but there was no longer anyone who could calm my fears.

Shouts awoke me the next morning and I opened my eyes to see a grey light shining through the tiny windows. The men who governed the ship walked among us, giving orders that most of us could not understand and using force to make their meaning clear.

They took us above deck one by one and splashed us with buckets of water from the sea—a pitiful excuse for bathing—and gave us hard bread and fresh water. Then one of the slavers, a thin man with a face like a weasel, translated into the Celtic tongue that we must clean the area where we were kept. We remained silent as we mopped up the filth from the wooden floor, none of us daring to question our captors.

Despite the outward submission, I felt a surge of hot anger bubble up inside me, and it took all of my strength to control it. That would bring punishment to all of us, but most of all to me. The injustice of the situation enraged me bitterly, and in my mind I screamed and cursed all of them—the Romans, the traders, even the very ship on which I was travelling. Having always been allowed great freedom, I gritted my teeth against this sudden yoke of bondage. I would not give up hope—not yet.

My father had often warned me against my fascination of the Roman kind, calling them instruments of evil. My brothers had never understood my feelings, and neither had Telyn. It was only now that I understood why my people detested the Redcrests, and oh! how I hated them, loathed them, despised them all.

In the days that followed, the child of the young mother who had spoken to me sickened in the crowded quarters of the ship's hold, dying before we reached the harbors of Rome. I watched in mute horror as the sailors casually wrapped the small form in canvas and tossed it overboard, ignoring the grieving shrieks of the mother. She cried her bairn's name over and over until they silenced her with threats of punishment. Then she sat in the corner, rocking back and forth with her arms wrapped around her body, the name *Ewen* escaping her lips in a whispered lament as tears streamed down her face.

No one dared comfort her, as we were forbidden to speak to one another, but more than one person looked at her with unspeakable pity in their eyes. Only I remained motionless, in shock at the mindless cruelty.

It was then that I knew Rome was a force beyond reckoning. I was only a girl, soon to be a slave, powerless against the enemies of my people. All that I had loved had been taken from me and I had little hope left in life. I could not fight for my freedom—I could not even save myself from my fate. I could do only one thing against those who had enslaved me: resist the temptation to let go of life entirely.

That was why I held on. Deep within my heart, even as I nurtured my hatred of the Roman people, I hoped that it would be better someday—that I would, against all odds, return home.

Bitterness and hope. A strange combination, but it was the only thing that sustained me—for it was better than nothing at all.

CHAPTER III

R OME!'

The cry echoed from the top deck and resounded into the depths of the ship. I still knew little of the Latin tongue, but that word I understood clearly. We captives awoke from sleep at the sound; the sun was rising in the east, and as I rubbed the last remnants of sleep from my eyes, I began to wonder what would now become of me.

Rome.

The very word filled me with a strange mixture of terror and curiosity. I was afraid of Rome—what might happen to me in that place. The fate of Boudicca's daughters crossed my mind, and my heart pounded. Even should I be spared similar mistreatment, I feared I would be given to a harsh master. Fate had not been kind to me thus far; why should I think it would go well with me now?

Yet oft I had heard tales from passing traders of the great Eternal City. A place, they said, of culture and literature, the arts and sciences; words that were almost meaningless to me, but I longed to know what they meant. Little had I known then that I would have not long to wait.

Sometime later—for every passing moment seemed to last an eternity—the ship docked at the harbor of Rome. We heard a great scrambling and shouting of orders, but knew nothing of what it meant. Then men came down and untied the ropes that bound our ankles and wrists, leading us up on the deck.

The sea air combined with city stench nigh overwhelmed me, and I felt lost, overcome by the roar of the populace. The city seemed to last forever, buildings upon buildings stretching for leagues, rising up on hills and extending into the far distances. Around us were ships of all sorts and sizes. Behind us, beyond the choked harbor, was the rolling blue ocean, its waves sparkling beneath the morning sun. I had never seen anything this large and grand; Venta Icenorum, though seen from a distance, had seemed to me immense, but it was nowhere near as colossal as this great capital of the Redcrests' empire.

My wonder did not last long. I was brought back to the present by being roughly hustled off the ship and onto the docks with my fellow slaves. Chains were locked around our wrists and ankles in place of the ropes that had once bound us. Our shackles were connected into one line as we were marched off like animals for the butcher, the slave dealer leading the way and his men goading us along. The ground was strangely firm after the pitching surface of the ship, and my first steps were mostly stumbling on smooth pavement.

Despite my fears of the near future, I gazed in amazement at my new surroundings. I had always imagined what a city built by the Redcrests must be like, but all my speculations fell utterly short of the reality.

The farther we traveled from the low hovels by the docks, the greater the buildings became. The roads were smooth, straight, and broad, with raised stones across the streets connecting walkways on either side, allowing both passersby and chariots to travel without difficulty. High buildings reared up into the sky on either side of the street, surrounded by shops on the ground level and living quarters further up. I had never before seen a structure with more than one floor, and I marveled at the strange phenomenon. What sort of people were so great as to create such things? 'Twas no wonder they called my people crude barbarians.

As we drew closer to the grand Forum in the middle of the city, the architecture became more refined. Beautiful temples and government buildings adorned the streets; and high up on the hills, rising from the humid and populous valleys, lay dazzling mansions that shone in the sunlight. What sort of place—be it humble shanty or golden palace—would I soon call my new home?

People of every sort brushed past us with never a second glance; people with pale skin like my own, people with the olive skin and ink-black hair of the Romans, and others with darker complexions that I could never have imagined.

When we came to the Forum, I gasped in surprise. All I had seen and wondered at paled in comparison. Temples and governmental buildings stood at the fringes of the vast open space, statues and monumental arches placed through the center, along with booths and stalls selling anything one could possibly want and more. However, when I laid eyes on one of the many stalls exhibiting slaves, my heart stopped and I was overcome by a burning wave of shame as my mind refused to acknowledge what would soon happen to me.

We were hustled into an enclosed area much like an animal pen while the slave dealer left his men to watch us and hustled over to a Roman official. They spoke together for some time, but I could not hear what they said. Instead, a voice screamed out in my mind against the atrocities of Rome. It was said to be a place of great culture; the buildings we had passed were evidence of this. But how could they call my people barbarians? We treated our bondmen with more dignity than this! White-hot rage seethed within me and I gritted my teeth. Could my gaze have melted marble, the entire empire would have vanished under a single glance.

The slave trader returned and gave orders to his men as they scurried around, preparing his stall for opening. He looked us over, clicking his tongue as his eyes raked our disheveled forms. Most of us stared at the ground or looked blankly at the distant horizon, but I gazed at him hotly, wishing to break free from my chains and escape what was to come. After a few minutes, he selected a few slaves and unlinked them from the rest of us, stripping them of their clothes and their dignity, leading them to the front of his market stall. Inwardly, I whispered prayers to the gods of my people that I would somehow be spared, but I had little hope. Gone were my thoughts of wonder and amazement at the glorious architecture of Rome; in their place were dread and loathing.

'Twas early in the morning, but already the marketplace was crowded with people of all classes. The noises of animals and thronging people filled the air, and above that cacophonous din rose the cries of merchants screaming out their wares to the people, begging them to come to their stalls and purchase their valuables. It was one thing to hear of such happenings, but quite another to see it and stand in the midst of the drama.

Our master seemed to be a well-kept and self-respecting slave merchant—if such a thing existed in this broken world—for only the wealthy patricians sought his wares to glorify their households, and he had long since disposed of those of us who were sick or had physical defects. One by one, the slaves standing before the crowd were bought and replaced by others. My heart hammered in my throat, fearing I would be next.

The sun rose higher into the sky, and soon sweat rolled freely down my brow. I dreaded every passing moment, every potential buyer who stopped and haggled with our trader, every slave who was sold and led off, for the time drew closer and closer when I too would be publicly shamed.

When the moment came and I was deprived of my clothes and whatever self-worth I had left, I felt no emotion. I had imagined being filled with rage enough to break my bonds and slay my captors. Yet I felt only a cold burning and held my gaze to the sky, staring at the clouds instead of the people who passed by. I could not—I dared not—think of anything but how blue the spring sky was. I could not have borne the shame otherwise.

I heard, as if at a great distance, voices heatedly discussing prices, some turning away, others arguing on. At last, I was purchased by a Roman matron nearly hidden from view by the silken curtains of an ornate litter, carried by four slaves and shadowed by her steward. She motioned for them to give me a cloak to hide my shame in—for which I was grateful—and I followed them with bowed head through the crowded streets, the heated pavement burning my bare feet.

The slaves bearing the litter labored in the hot sun, slowly toiling up one of the seven hills in the city. As we ascended, the buildings became increasingly spread out, the white marble villas glistening in the sunlight, surrounded by gardens, some public, many private. I could see little in detail of these homes for the upper classes of Roman society, but I had not long to wait before I was swept up against my will and made a part of the household.

I padded after the bent and sweating backs of the slaves before me as we made our way past the gates that bordered the grounds of the Aurelian villa and across the broad marble path that led to the mansion's doors. There they bent down and lowered the litter to the ground, allowing the lady of the house to step out, her golden jewelry sparkling in the sunlight. She beckoned for them to carry the litter away and then she looked at me. No words left her mouth; she only crooked her finger, gesturing for me to follow her and the steward into the grand mansion that loomed above us.

The cool dimness of the *atrium* was disorienting after the blinding brightness of the sun, and I squeezed my eyes shut until I could see in the darkness. Light spilled down from an opening in the roof, splashing golden rays on the still waters of a small pool directly below. Around the atrium were several closed doors, and at the far end lay a small shrine encasing various Roman gods and goddesses. Beautiful mosaics formed an odd texture beneath my bare feet as I clutched the cloak tightly around me and followed my mistress beyond the atrium, through a small passageway, and back out into the sunlight of the *peristylium*.

The peristylium was an elaborately landscaped garden surrounded by a marble colonnade supporting an inwardly sloping roof of terracotta tile. Fountains bubbled merrily, and within the walls of the house, the sound of the city was shut out. The peristylium, like the atrium, was surrounded by doors, and windows looking down into the garden courtyard from a second story.

As I looked around, some of that dread that had filled my heart an hour before dissipated. Perhaps it would not be so bad after all. I was no longer free, but at least my new home was very fine compared to what I was used to. I could only hope that my mistress would not be as cruel and barbaric as many other Romans seemed to be.

My thoughts were interrupted by the arrival of several female figures who came at the lady's call. The heat of the city had vanished behind the marble walls of the villa, and I shivered beneath the cover of the thin cloak as my fears of the unknown resurfaced.

The lady of the house spoke many words in a crisp voice, a voice that reminded me of my own mother when she was displeased. But I understood none of them until she gestured to her steward, who translated into broken Celtic, 'Thou wilt follow these women and do as they bid thee.'

I nodded and followed them out of the peristylium into a room beyond. It was bare save for the rolled sleeping mats stacked against the wall and some ropes hanging from the ceiling. I watched in curiosity as the slave women busied themselves, some gathering bottles of coloured liquids, others filling a large bronze basin with steaming hot water.

Then I realized they meant to wash me. Though I longed to be clean of the filth from the voyage, I recoiled at the thought of abandoning the privacy of the cloak. One might think me mad, for had I not been so disgraced before the whole of Roman people thronging the marketplace? But I supposed I did not want to have to endure more of such shame than necessary.

I was not given much of a choice.

The women tore the cloak from me and all but deposited me in the bronzen tub. I hated being exposed in such a way to them, but I had no choice but to submit myself to their rigorous scrubbing and untangling of my scarlet locks.

When at last I passed their inspection for cleanliness, one of them silently led me back to the atrium. I walked stiffly, slowly adjusting to the strange feel of a tunic around my body and sandals on my feet. I had always gone barefoot, and the leather bound around my feet felt like iron chains. My hair had been combed and pulled away from my face in a simple design; it felt odd not to have to thrust it back from my eyes all the time. Yet as different as the new clothing felt against my skin, at least I was clean again.

The slave woman motioned for me to stay, then walked away, her footsteps echoing in the quiet house.

As soon as she was gone, I stepped forward and looked at my broken reflection in the rippling waters of the atrium pool. I did not like what I saw, for it was a blank face, void of expression. Yet that was how it had to be, for unless my father and my brothers and Telyn searched all the ends of the world for me, I would not be returning home any time soon.

My memories were precious to me. I did not want them stolen as well, so I locked them away and feigned ignorance. It was the only way I could go on.

All I had left was hope.

CHAPTER IV

I HEARD VOICES and turned my head to look at the entrance to the great villa of Aurelius. Two young girls, whom I assumed to be near my own age, appeared in the dimness of the atrium. Retreating to the shadows, I watched as they stepped lightly across the mosaic floor, their finely-woven tunics fluttering with the delicacy of a butterfly. They were excitedly discussing something—though I understood none of it—and they laughed often, a ringing sound that echoed in the nigh empty atrium.

Then the lady of the house entered, the warm rays of the sun splashing light on the shimmering gold threads of her saffron *stola*. With her was her steward. The girls stopped talking and would have left, had not the matron indicated for them to stay. At that gesture, I stepped out of the shadows.

They were startled by my presence. One of them began speaking to the mistress, but she hushed the girl by raising her hand and spoke to me instead, her steward translating. 'My name is Honoria. This is my steward, Dennis. Thou art now part of the household of Aurelius Augustus Trajan. Thy past life thou must forget; thy new name is Marcella—'

I recoiled as if I had been slapped across the face. Was it not enough that they had taken everything from me? Must they also take my name?

Honoria did not seem to notice my slight movement and continued speaking. 'Thou must forget thy mother tongue and learn the Latin to understand our commands. If thou showest any sign of rebellion, we will not have mercy. Our household has no place for disobedient servants. Thou wilt be maidservant to my daughter, Aurelia.' She held out her hand towards one of the two girls, who only stared at me with wide, dark eyes. 'Thou wilt obey her every command; and if thou dost not, rest assured, I shall hear of it. The rest of thy duties thou wilt learn in time. Dost thou understand?'

I nodded slowly, feeling the invisible weight of servanthood descend upon my shoulders like the heavy yoke on a brace of oxen. The resurging pain of despair ached in my chest, but I could do nothing to relieve it.

'Now go. She will instruct thee.' Honoria turned on her heel and left. Dennis bowed his head to the daughter and left also, his sandals slapping away across the mosaic floor.

I swallowed hard and looked at Aurelia, wondering what sort of person my new mistress was.

She opened her mouth and closed it, still staring at me. She whispered something to her companion and waited for a reply. Then she spoke to me, and to my relief, I knew enough Latin by now to understand. 'Come ye, Marcella.' The words were spoken innocently enough, but with an edge of cool disdain. It was clear she thought me beneath her, but then, what did I expect? I was no longer a chieftain's daughter, but a slave and barbarian.

Aurelia walked away, holding her friend's hand. Obediently, I followed a few paces behind them, feeling as though somehow I was walking away from my old self, exchanging Enid of the Iceni for Marcella, maidservant to Aurelia. There was no escape, no way for me to go back; what was lost was lost forever. I had no choice but to move on.

The two girls often looked over their shoulder at me, exchanging whispers and giggles. Stepping out into the peristylium, I saw Aurelia as more than the colourful, wispy shape I had discerned in the darkness of the atrium. The sunlight glanced off her shining black hair and smooth olive skin. Her dark eyes sparkled in the brilliance of day and I thought her very pretty, despite my intentions to despise all Romans.

They led me into a windowless room lit by oil lamps that I supposed to be Aurelia's bedchamber. The mosaic tiling continued and brightly-coloured frescoes adorned the walls. A gilded table displayed various items from expensive perfumes to jeweled combs for hair, though Aurelia could not yet adorn herself as a married woman. Her bed lay opposite, a fairly simple affair for a wealthy household, but I soon learned that simple beds were the custom save in the imperial palace.

Once in the shelter of Aurelia's room, the two girls took off their dusty sandals and put on ones similar to mine—house-sandals, I guessed. On their ankles, the girls each wore a leather strap on which hung a small silver crescent.

Aurelia's companion quickly tied on her own shoes, but Aurelia slipped hers on both feet and held them out for me to fasten, pointing to them and saying '*Solea.*'

Swallowing my pride—for I did not doubt that Honoria's threats about rebellious servants were meant in earnest—I knelt down and tied Aurelia's solea, my fingers awkwardly knotting the strings. My clumsiness made the girls laugh and my face burned with humiliation, though I tried to hide it.

When they left the room, Aurelia gestured for me to stay. Closing the door behind them, they left me in silence.

For some time, I gazed around the room, taking in every minuscule detail so as to memorize the position of every object. Eventually, I grew tired of standing and sat on the cold floor, for I assumed a slave would not be permitted to sit on the bed or the chair before the gilded table.

I leaned my head against the frescoed wall and stared at the dim shadows of the ceiling high above me. I could scarce believe I had only this morning been on the ship that carried me from my home. It seemed so long ago.

The flickering light from the oil lamps elongated the shadows on the walls and ceiling and my gaze blurred, seeing only the orange and black merging together in a trembling dance....

The sun sank into the west, casting lengthy shadows over the golden carpet of dried leaves. The air was crisp and cool and the wind was still, as if holding its breath, waiting for something to happen. I stood up on the hill, gazing at my village in the valley below, feeling the papery bark of birch through the thin sleeve of my tunic. Soon, it would be time for me to return for the evening feast of Mabon.

I closed my eyes, feeling the warmth of the autumn day slip away into the cold of the coming darkness. I heard a slight scuffling—a rabbit jumping across the leaves, perhaps.

Someone's hand locked down on my eyes and a moment later their lips met mine. Warmth swept through my being and I reached up to pull the unknown hand away.

With a lightning-fast movement, his hand was gone.

I spun around to see a dark-haired figure bounding away down the hill. He turned to glance behind him and in that half-breath of a moment, I recognized Telyn's face.

I smiled, feeling as though my body would burst for sheer happiness. I ran after him, the memory of that kiss seared into my mind forever....

I woke with a start and gazed around in disoriented panic before the events of the day came rushing back. For the first time, an aching lump rose in my throat and cold tears trickled down my face. I brushed them away angrily. I wanted to cry, to weep without restraint, to grieve the loss of everything that had been mine and never would be mine again. Yet I was afraid of being shamed if Aurelia returned to the room at that moment.

Rubbing my face hard, I rose stiffly to my feet. My empty stomach rumbled. Would I be noticed if I slipped out of the room?

I decided against it. I had been commanded to stay put, and the bondwomen might think ill of me for escaping and begging for food. I was now dependent upon the whims of my mistress, a hard thing for someone who had once been as free and untamable as the birds in the forest. Untamable I remained, but my freedom had been forfeited.

It made me wish—almost—that Telyn had never asked to speak with me. For aye, I would not know that he wished to wed me, but at least I would be home and safe and free. I wondered whether they had taken Telyn too, or if they had killed him. Or perhaps he had escaped only to discover I was missing. What did my family think? Had they searched for me, or had they given me up as one of the dead?

The door opened and Aurelia stepped into the room. Her smile vanished as she caught sight of me and she said something that I did not understand. It did not sound like a command, for it was spoken quietly, as if to herself.

'Marcella.'

I stared at her in confusion for several seconds until I remembered that Marcella was my new name. Enid was no more. My mind worked furiously in hopes I would comprehend whatever she would say next.

She pointed to her hair and then to the comb.

I nearly laughed at the outrageousness of it. It stood to reason that a young woman of her age should be able to tie her own sandals and comb her own hair, but no. I must needs be stolen from my home and everything I loved to do it for her.

Aurelia sat down stiffly on the chair, the folds of her tunic settling prettily around her. I picked up the comb, undid the simple hairstyle, and ran the teeth of the comb through the sable strands, my fingers gently working out any tangles. When I finished, she remained sitting, and I realized I must do something with the inky locks as well.

Sighing inwardly, I began to braid, hoping my simple style would be to her liking. I attempted to copy the Roman pattern the women had woven into my own hair, but with a British twist. Despite my efforts, it looked nothing like I had hoped, but at least it was neat.

Aurelia rose to her feet and spoke slowly, her hands gesturing. I supposed her message to be along the lines of, 'Go to the kitchens and eat,' for I recognized the Latin word for food, and the word *culina*, or kitchen, had been spoken to me earlier. Then she departed for the dining room while I made my way across the darkening peristylium to the kitchens.

The evening was dull. After eating what food the servants gave me—which was nothing I wished to eat, but hunger forbade me to go without—I returned to Aurelia's chamber and waited for her return. An hour or so later I helped her prepare for bed, and she sent me to sleep with the other slave women. Fortunately, I remembered how to find the room where they had bathed me, and I found a space among them to lie down.

Despite my weariness, sleep was far from me. An ache still weighed on my chest, a need to burst forth in violent weeping. Tears longed to fall. All I wished was to go back in time and replay my actions, to somehow change my miserable fate. I glanced up at the ceiling above me, at the sleeping bodies around me, and one solitary tear slipped down my face. Since my captivity, even my dreams haunted me, taunting me with what had been, what might have been, and what now would never be. Yet here I was, suspended between two worlds: the world I loved and the hateful world I was a part of whether I wanted it or not.

I wished to go back home, to wake up and realize it had all been some terrible dream. But as I rolled onto my side and closed my weary eyes, I recognized in my heart of hearts that perhaps there was to be no return for me.

CHAPTER V

THE NEXT MORNING dawned silver-grey and cold. 'Twas the cold that woke me first. The damp seeped in through my thin slave's tunic, and I opened my eyes to the dimness of morning. Around me, the other slave women were preparing for the day, washing their hair and braiding it.

I sat up, shivering, my mouth parched. As I did not know how to communicate with them, I remained silent. Several of them left, and I rose to my feet, thinking perhaps I should follow them, but I did not know where. Aurelia had not explained anything to me the previous day, and even if she had, I could not fully understand her.

Swallowing hard, I approached one of the bondwomen and questioned in a small voice, 'What am I supposed to do?'

She did not answer me, but turned around and spoke to the others, laughing.

My face burned in humiliation. I turned away and unbraided my hair, running my fingers through the scarlet strands and attempting to forget their presence.

The door swung open and the titters of the women and girls were hushed as they filed out in respectful silence. I glanced up and came face to face with one of my fellow slave women, much older than the others, strands of greying yellow hair escaping the coil on her head. 'Marcella?' The voice attached to the speaker reminded me of my mother. Not in the way Honoria's did, for that similarity was only in displeasure. But this was in timbre and compassion, which no one in this strange place had yet shown me.

I nodded my head in reply, my stomach beginning to growl in hunger. I wondered if perhaps I should get to my feet instead of sitting on the floor.

The slave straightened from bending over me and pointed a stubby finger towards herself. '*Ego Agrippinam,*' she said slowly.

I blinked in confusion. When she repeated her words and still I did not show any signs of understanding, she pointed to me and articulated quite clearly, 'Marcella.' Then pointing to herself once more, she said only, 'Agrippina.'

I gestured towards her and imitated her word, 'Agrippina,' assuming it to be her name.

Agrippina smiled, nodding her head. '*Ita.*'

I took that to be the Redcrests' way of saying aye, and repeated it. The word felt strange on my tongue. The orderly language of my masters was vastly different from the deep-throated and melodic speech of my own kind. Even if I had the intelligence to pick it up quickly, a part of me abhorred the thought of speaking Latin—as if in doing so I would lose yet another thread that bound me to my old world.

'Come, Marcella,' Agrippina said, reaching out to take my hand in her worn, calloused one. She led me to the kitchens and motioned for me to sit down with the other slaves, who were hastily swallowing down what they called pottage, a soup of boiled vegetables and grains. It tasted terrible to me, but it was warm and I was too hungry to care.

After I broke my fast, Agrippina took me to Aurelia's room and knocked. Hearing a reply, I looked nervously to Agrippina, unsure of what I was supposed to do. She opened the door and gently nudged me inside. As her footsteps faded away, a minuscule surge of panic rose in my throat. How was I supposed to understand what to do without someone patient and willing to explain everything to me?

Aurelia pushed aside her bedclothes and placed a tray in my hands. It bore remnants of what I supposed was her breakfast, though it looked quite different from the strange pottage we slaves had eaten. She pointed to the door and spoke to me, though I only understood one word: *culina*, the kitchen.

I returned to the kitchens and gave the tray to Agrippina before hastening back, my sandals padding softly on the dewy mosaics.

Aurelia placed a small stack of garments in my hands and gestured for me to follow her out into the atrium. There her mother waited for us, a look of mild annoyance on her face. I felt horribly guilty, supposing I had delayed them.

We walked out into the morning sun, the shining gold on the buildings in the Forum nearly blinding my eyes. I was unaccustomed to the bustle and hurry and crowded confines of a city. The streets were fairly quiet on the Esquiline, the hill where the Aurelian villa lay, but once we came to the lower sections of the city in the valleys between the seven hills, the noise increased. Farmers rushed to have their carts outside the city walls before the day grew any later, and already the Forum was crowded with people. But we passed them by, heading in the direction of the Roman baths.

A tall, ornate building, much like the others, towered above the wide street. A stream of women and girls entered in, chattering excitedly, the wealthier ones trailed by female slaves. I looked with wide eyes at the marble columns and high-arched ceilings above me as echoes of words and laughter rose in the air, disappearing among the birds' nests resting on the leaves of the intricately-carved Corinthian pillars. What beauty the Redcrests were capable of creating! My own people would never have dreamed of making such elegant edifices.

Awkwardly copying the other slaves of the Aurelian household, I sat down on one of many marble benches in a large open room. Aurelia and her mother disappeared behind small doors and reemerged wearing nothing, leaving their old garments in our hands with the fresh ones.

Shocked and speechless, I hardly dared watch as they went with many others into another wide room, out of which escaped steam. My people had no such grand buildings in which to bathe, but even we had more modesty. I would never have washed in the stream in front of anyone, not even my own sisters; but these Romans did not seem to mind.

I do not know how long it took for Honoria and her daughter to return to us, for the minutes seemed to drag on forever. My thoughts wandered aimlessly, the only thing clear to me that freedom still seemed tantalizingly near—so near I could almost touch it.

Then an idea occurred to me, an idea that I could not thrust away no matter how hard I tried. If I appeared as if I was simply going to look out at the street, I could slip away and be gone within minutes. And with all the other people wandering about the streets this time of day, they would never find me.

Glancing at the other slaves, who all seemed on the verge of dropping asleep or were talking to one another, I laid aside the garments on the side of the bench and rose to my feet, ignoring my racing heart. Walking slowly to the archways a few corridors down, I leaned against one of the smooth pillars and looked out at the busy street where pedestrians brushed each other's shoulders and a boy chased an escaped chicken. Some distance away, the Roman patrol came marching down the street, the populace parting before them as water breaks before a stone in the stream.

I cast a glance over my shoulder and saw one of Honoria's slaves coming towards me. I did not know why the slave was walking towards me, but my heart jumped into my throat and I lost my senses. Freedom was almost within my reach—I could not bear to lose it again. Panicked, I dove down the stairs from the baths and jostled my way through the street, ignoring people's cries and attempts to stop my flight.

Someone grabbed my arm, nearly jerking it out of its socket as I tried to wrench free. Whirling around, I came face to face with one of the Roman patrol. The face beneath the gilded helmet revealed that he was scarcely more than a boy. But what surprised me more than his youth was his resemblance to Telyn: the same high forehead and cheekbones, the same jet-black brows, and the same proud mouth.

I stared at him, too shocked to renew my escape attempt, and he stared back at me wide-eyed, as if he also recognized my features, though we had never met before. He opened his mouth to speak, but it was too late.

The slave woman grabbed my other arm, yanking me out of the boy's grasp, and she started shouting at me, slapping my face with her hand. It stung badly, but the pain was not so great as the sinking feeling in my chest. Gone was the pulsing frenzy in my veins; in its place was stony dread. I looked beyond the slave gripping me tightly as the Roman patrol marched on, but the youth did not turn around.

Still berating me though I understood nothing she said, the woman dragged me up the stairs to the baths and made me sit on the floor, her heavy, sweaty hand holding onto my shoulder in case I should try to escape again. I was silent and sullen, too ashamed to cry in front of the others.

When Honoria and Aurelia finally came back and dressed, I began to arrange Aurelia's hair in the same style I had the night before while the two listened to the slave woman tell of my failed escape. My ears burned, but I kept quiet—not that they would have been able to understand my protests or explanations.

The woman finished and I glanced up to see Honoria give me a sharp look. My heart sank to my feet. Any thought of mercy vanished under her withering gaze. Shrinking even further within myself, I kept my head bowed as we returned to the sunlight and open air, feeling nothing but the desperate throbbing of my heart.

The Forum was a blaze of colour, the roar of the merchants' voices dizzyingly loud as they cried their wares around us. I felt sick amid the ocean of noise beneath a blazing sun, but I had to follow Aurelia's footsteps like a hound on a leash, unable to escape.

Then I caught sight of someone standing only a few booths away and the world stopped.

Telyn.

I stared at him, stunned, as he looked around the Roman Forum, seeming lost, as I was, in this strange new world. The sight of him brought back the bitterness of my loss, and the desire to break free and run to him was painful. Unconsciously I pulled away from the group, only to be called back by a sharp word from Honoria. I called out to him, shouting his name over and over until a box on the ears from Honoria silenced me—but it was useless. My voice was lost among the clamor.

I craned my neck to gaze behind me, putting to memory Telyn's face, the last symbol of home in this foreign land. He searched the marketplace, looking for me—for why else would he be here?—but his eyes always missed me. I wanted to burst into tears, to scream against the unfairness of it. He was so close, and yet so far away.

He was soon lost to my view, and I knew I would not see him again. My only opportunity had slipped from my grasp even as I reached for it. And there were no such things in life as second chances.

CHAPTER VI

LTHOUGH I EXPECTED no mercy at Honoria's hands, I was not prepared for the ferocity of my punishment. Once we arrived back at the Aurelian villa, she grabbed me by my wrist and pulled me into the room where I had slept the night before. I fell onto the floor, the smooth stones skinning my knees, and she turned and barked out commands to the slave women who loitered near, watching. I heard footsteps fade away and then return, but I did not look up. I trembled in terrified anticipation and my stomach twisted itself in knots.

Two of the slaves pulled me to my feet and positioned me facing the wall. I knew what was going to happen next, but I was powerless to stop it. The neck of my tunic was loosened and pulled down to my waist, my hands tied to ropes dangling from the ceiling—I now understood the purpose of those ropes. I clenched my teeth as the slave women left me, bracing myself for the blows soon to follow.

I heard rather than felt the crack of the whip in the beginning; the strange snap sounded like thunder in my ears. I had witnessed many such punishments in Britain, but until now I had never been the victim. When the pain began, it felt like fire snaking across my skin, burning as though someone had thrust a torch through me. I could not keep back the tears, but I refused to scream. Blood pounded in my ears as the crack of the whip slowly faded away beneath the pain.

It seemed to go on forever, though in reality it did not last long. I heard Honoria give commands to someone who loosened my bonds. Then she walked away and the door closed behind her.

I sank to the floor, turning my head to reassure myself that I was alone. Beyond the door, the household resumed its daily duties, leaving me forgotten. Tears spilled down my cheeks and my back burned, hot blood slowly trickling down, tickling my broken skin. But my rage was gone. The white-hot anger that had simmered within me only moments before when I made my escape had vanished into a lifeless mist, like the finished weapon that the swordsmith plunges into the bucket of water, the once-glowing blade emerging from the steam a dull black.

Even if escape were possible, my chances of returning to my homeland were almost none. I would be hunted down the moment I fled the house, and the possibility of survival in Rome wearing a slave's tunic and possessing little knowledge of the

Latin tongue was slim indeed. And should I be caught again, my punishment would only be greater.

It was a cruel fate that had kept Telyn from hearing me, from seeing me. In my mind, the scene played over and over again with haunting clarity. So close to touching him—not just a symbol of home, but someone I loved. So close to freedom. If only I had shouted louder! If only I had wrestled loose and run to him! Surely he would not have let me be stolen away again. If only I had waited to run until we were in the Forum. If only! If only! If only!

I squeezed my eyes shut, the last of the tears slipping out at the corners and down my dampened face. It was useless to hide from reality, yet I feared the future. I did not want to forget my past and my people, but how could I hold onto them and still meekly accept the yoke of slavery? A scream rose in my throat, but it came out as a pitiful whimper. It felt like death, though my body was alive and knew it all too well.

The door creaked open. I wished to be left alone, but I no longer had a choice in such matters.

'Marcella!'

Agrippina bent over me, clicking her tongue as she looked at the broken, bleeding skin on my back. She pulled me to my feet and took me with her to the kitchen while I rubbed my face hard as if to hide the traces of tears. I felt numb, my motions automatic. My back was horribly stiff and continued to burn, a dull and distant throbbing compared to the sharp ache in my heart.

The culina was empty, for at this hour most were taking their afternoon rest during the hottest time of the day—for which I was glad, as I did not want company. Agrippina bade me sit on the table in the center of the kitchen and I held my tunic so that only my back was bare. She spoke soothingly to me in her own native tongue as she bustled about boiling water and gathering herbs and bandages. I understood none of her words, but her voice calmed some of the turmoil within me.

She pressed cool, wet cloths gently against the wounds. I sucked in my breath sharply as my skin smarted, but said nothing. The cold water numbed my back and I closed my eyes as she proceeded to grind a mixture and add hot water to create a paste. The pungent odor of the crushed herbs tickled my senses and my nose twitched at its unfamiliarity. There were such women gifted in healing in my village, but I had not spent enough time in their bothies to become acquainted with the different plants and their uses.

Agrippina loosened my grip on my tunic and applied the paste to the lacerations, an icy sting spreading through my back as the herbs met my raw wounds. The pain was less now, but the stiffness remained. I wondered if this was to be my last beating or if it was only a forerunner of what was to come.

Then Agrippina spoke to me in the clipped Latin, repeating her words slowly and gesturing to show me the meaning. One word she repeated often: '*Dormire.*' By the way she folded her hands together and placed them by her head, closing her eyes each time, I took it to mean sleep.

She led me back to the room where I had been whipped. Obediently, I lay down, wincing as each movement stretched my wounded back and sent new spasms of pain across it. The cook smiled sadly, a look of pity in her eyes as she looked at me before closing the door.

I felt strangely weary, as if all the events of the last two hours had sapped the last of my strength. I was broken, all remnants of a fight for freedom gone.

I heard someone singing beyond the door, but the words were lost to me and the melody soon faded away as I slipped into a fitful and dreamless sleep.

I opened my eyes some hours later, my head pounding and my mouth terribly dry. I sat up, realizing too late that such movements would have to be handled with care while my back healed.

I rose slowly and awkwardly to my feet and stumbled to the door, still feeling half asleep. Meandering to the kitchens, I found Agrippina shouting at other slaves as they busied themselves with dinner preparations. I gestured my need for a drink of water and was promptly given one and told to stand in the corner so as not to be in the way. As my head cleared, I watched with interest as several of them quickly chopped vegetables and others prepared bread and meat to be baked or roasted in the large ovens. I could have watched them for much longer had Honoria not summoned me to the atrium.

I made my way across the peristylium as the sun began to sink into the west, scarlet and gold rays of light striking the marble pillars so that they looked as if they were made of molten metal. The air was humid and still, and sweat formed on my forehead.

The atrium was already lit by oil lamps, and with the dying light of the sun falling through the opening in the roof, I could clearly see Honoria and Dennis standing there, waiting for me. I knew what they were going to say.

Even though it was Dennis' translation, Honoria's emphasis and fluctuations of her voice were only too clear.

'I hope thou dost understand that there are to be no further escape attempts. Whatever thy life has been before, it is over. Thou belongest to us, and as a slave, thou art to be obedient. If thou triest again to flee this house and thy good masters, the punishment will be worse. Dost thou understand?'

I swallowed hard, utterly defeated. I looked down at the mosaic floor, the blues and reds blurring together, and nodded my head, the last remnants of my rebellious spirit fleeing away.

'Good. Now return to thy room. I wish thee to rest before resuming thy duties with Aurelia.'

I nodded again and turned away, slipping away into the silence of the slave women's room. I lay down, my eyes staring at the ceiling above me, but sleep did not come. I felt drained and empty, as heavy as if the weight of the ocean was on my shoulders, yet as shallow as a mere puddle filled with rainwater.

Beyond the door, people moved back and forth, the shadows of their footsteps stealing in through the space between the door and the floor. Eventually the sounds ceased to come from the peristylium and escaped the dining room instead. I knew Agrippina would be wanting me in the culina with the other slaves, but I did not feel hungry.

The light slowly died away. A bird sang in the garden. The chirping was muffled by the door, but as I listened, the song seemed to take on a life of its own, weaving up and down, and for a moment I was back home, listening to Caradoc pluck the strings of his harp. I minded how melancholy the melody had been—a lament, he called it. I wanted to cry, but I had no tears left. All that had been mine was gone beyond recall and only in dreams could I ever hope to reclaim it.

The song suddenly stopped and I sat up, hearing someone approaching the door. It was Agrippina. Without words spoken between us, I rose to my feet and followed her down to the kitchens.

I was no longer Enid of the Iceni; I was Marcella, a Roman slave. I had a new life, a new name now. The past had to be buried, for it was no more.

PART II

I keep making peace with the past
Then the present won't let me
Thought the memories were buried so deep
Envy takes over
That should be me
All it took is one look and I fall apart

CHAPTER VII

TIME WOULD FAIL me to speak of the infinitesimal happenings of my life during the four years that followed the beginning of my slavery in Rome. Suffice it to say that I succeeded—almost—in burying the past. My mistresses were just, and as long as I obeyed and remained as a blank and living statue, I received no more beatings. I learned the Romans' Latin, but in my heart I still clung to my mother tongue, though all else that had been Enid was replaced by Marcella. Rarely would I let myself dream of my home, of my family, of Telyn. It hurt too much to remember. For when I did think of them, my heart was overborne with such longing and pain that I feared it would break. So I shut them away, locked deep within my heart, far from the light of day.

As for the Aurelian household, many changes had taken place. A year since I became maidservant to Aurelia, Emperor Vespasian of Rome died and his son Titus peacefully succeeded him. The same year, Mount Vesuvius erupted, destroying the cities of Pompeii, Herculaneum, Oplontis, and Stabiae, and various other settlements nearby. Many relatives of Aurelius perished in the disaster, and the family grieved them for months. Almost three years later, Emperor Titus died of fever, and his brother, Domitian, replaced him. As a slave, these things mattered little to me in the grand scheme of life, but to the family of Aurelius, as well as many other Romans, they were of great importance.

'Marcella! Marcella!'

A vigorous smacking of my face brought me out of a dreamless sleep to reality and I sat up with a jerk, meeting the face of Agrippina.

'Marcella, why dost thou sleep so late?' She straightened with a huff and looked at me mournfully. 'Why canst thou not rise early after all these years?'

I struggled to my feet and yawned, the remnants of sleep fleeing away. Running my fingers through my hair, I realized that I would have to wash later as I had arisen too late to do it now. I staggered to the kitchen and washed down a few mouthfuls of pottage before scurrying around preparing Aurelia's breakfast.

Balancing a tray of bread with honey, cheese, olives, fruit, and a small glass of wine, I stepped out of the kitchen and into the peristylium. My sandaled feet made almost no noise on the mosaic floor, which was wet with morning dew beneath the roofed portions of the garden. Pale pink and grey light shone in the east as the sun began to break over the city of Rome, and I inhaled deeply the icy breath of dawn, shivering a little in my thin tunic.

I knocked on the door to Aurelia's quarters and leaned my ear against the smooth wood, listening for a reply.

'*Intrabit.*'

Gripping the tray hard with one hand, I turned the knob and entered the dimly-lit room, closing the door behind me with my heel.

'Thou art late this morn,' Aurelia said simply.

I nodded and placed the tray beside her, standing back with my hands clasped and waiting for orders.

'Well, what was the cause of it?' She reached for an olive and popped it into her mouth.

I was silent, listening to her chewing.

'Marcella, must we always play this game?' Aurelia put two olives in her mouth this time.

I kept my peace. It was always a battle with me, caught between ignoring her as if I was a dumb animal or speaking to her. She was the only one besides Agrippina who had ever tried to speak to me as a friend. Yet there were still times when I could not see the Romans as human beings, but only as the enemy—and silence was my only weapon.

Aurelia sighed heavily and continued eating, saying between mouthfuls, 'Prepare my clothes for the baths. Be sure to bring my finer *toga praetexta* for me to wear afterwards. My brother may be coming home on leave and perhaps he will bring one of his friends with him, as he is always promising to do.' She sighed again, this time dreamily, no doubt imagining in her mind a handsome soldier on whom to bestow her affections. Yet even I knew that soldiers could not marry until their time of service was up.

I nodded and went about her room, silently preparing her things.

After breaking her fast, Aurelia rose out of bed and waited patiently as I neatened her hair enough for walking the streets in the early hours of the dawn. Then I tied her *calceus*—outdoor sandals—on her feet, before picking up the bundle of items she had instructed me to bring with her and following her out of the house.

Honoria and her maidservants walked with us in silence. The sun had risen by this hour and its bright rays touched the golden domes and monuments all over the city, lighting gleaming little beacons that nearly blinded my eyes. The air was warmer, but still retained the fresh chill of early spring. However, the noise from the city was never-ending, and its thunderous roar met us as we descended the Esquiline Hill into the heart of the city.

Having reached the baths, I entered with the rest and sat down on a marble bench in the *apodyterium*, guarding the belongings of my mistress as she stripped and went into the *tepidarium*. Why anyone in their right mind would endure sweating out all the moisture in their body and then plunge into an icy pool, repeating the process every day, was beyond my understanding.

I leaned back against the wall, crossing my arms, and waited for Aurelia to finish. Fortunately, the clamour of the baths was loud enough that I was in no danger of falling asleep. Thieves regularly stole from the baths, and should I be guilty of not keeping watch, there would be little hope for mercy.

Sometimes, when I let my mind wander, I thought of the first time I had come to the baths and of my ill-fated escape attempt. Often, when we went to the Forum, I would look for Telyn, knowing even as I did so that I would not see him. Occasionally, I looked also for that Roman soldier who had reminded me so much of Telyn, but I never saw him either.

It seemed an eternity before Aurelia came out, took her clean clothes, and dressed. Then she sat down while I combed her hair and arranged it in her favorite design.

'*Mater*, may we go to the Forum before returning home?' Aurelia questioned, her voice sounding sickly sweet, like too much honey. She believed—probably rightly—that using such a submissive tone would increase her chances of getting her way.

I groaned inwardly. Aurelia could spend hours in the Forum, haggling with the merchants. I had scarcely eaten that morning and my stomach growled in hunger. I did not fancy the prospect of standing under the sun for hours, carrying my mistress's things.

'*Ita,* as long as thou art home in time for the midday meal.'

'*Gratias tibi, mea mater.*' Aurelia bowed her head meekly, but I was near enough to sense her trembling in excitement.

I followed her out under the glare of the golden star in the sky, carrying the bundle of items I knew I would be bearing for quite some time. Already the day was hot, and within moments, sweat rolled freely underneath my tunic.

The Forum was filled with people at this hour and merchants' voices screamed to the sky as beggars asked for alms in odd locations and poor children ran hither and thither. The air carried the smells of spices and human and animal odors. I wrinkled my nose in disgust and fought the urge to sneeze.

Aurelia cast eager eyes over the bracelets and other forms of jewelry at one booth, her hands fingering various pieces with interest. I thought little of them; my people had far more skill in metalworking than the Romans, and these jeweled pieces did not impress me.

'How much for this?' I heard my mistress say as she held up a silver necklace set with emeralds. A moment later, she and the merchant were locked in a fierce battle of bargaining.

My eyes wandered across the Forum. In the center of the immense plaza stood the Milliarium Aureum, the Golden Milestone erected by the first Roman Emperor, Augustus. It was a column sheathed in gold bronze, and upon it was engraved the names of chief cities and their distance from Rome. Of course, Venta Icenorum was not there, but Londinium was; Aurelia had shown it to me a few months after I had been enslaved. Many times in the first few years in Rome, I would go to it, my trembling fingers brushing over the word lovingly as I whispered to my family and Telyn how much I missed them and wished to return. But I did not do that anymore.

My gaze returned to Aurelia, who evidently had won her battle. With a triumphant smile, she handed over the bronze coins in exchange for the necklace, giving me the piece of jewelry to carry. To my relief, she did not linger any longer at any other of the stalls, but determinedly struck out for home, chattering all the while about how happy she was to have won her bargain.

I thought of her as somewhat of a silly girl, concerned only about parties and handsome young men and looking beautiful. Despite this shallowness, she was sincere in her attempts to befriend me. But there was a great divide between us, no matter how much she tried to cross it: I was a slave, she a senator's daughter. The Romans stood in my mind as a symbol of my slavery and separation from those I loved and I hated them for it; I could never see them as anything else.

'Marcella, I wish thou didst show more interest in these things.'

Hearing my name mentioned, I snapped my head up in attention.

'Mater says I should try to be more fashionable. But whenever I find pretty things, she never approves of them. She says they do not look well on me. Perhaps I should give them to thee. Wouldst thou like that?'

I shook my head, opening my mouth to speak. 'I am a slave; 'tis not my place to adorn myself in such finery.'

She shook her head. 'Thou art impossible. I try to be kind, but thou must always remind me that thou art a slave. Can we not forget it between us?'

Having opened my mouth once, I found it hard not to continue speaking. 'Aurelia, do not be foolish. Even if I cared about trivial matters such as clothing—and jewels—and fine young men, I could not discuss them with thee. I am a slave. 'Tis my duty to look after thy needs, nothing more.'

Aurelia stopped walking and looked me full in the face, her dark eyes glimmering with tears about to fall. 'Dost thou truly not care?' Her voice was soft, like the whisper of a butterfly in flight.

I shrugged my shoulders. 'Why should I? They mean nothing to me.'

'Oh!' She turned away from me, her shoulders slumped, and she continued on her way, this time setting a brisker pace.

I shadowed her, my head bowed as befitted my rank as we toiled up the slopes of the Esquiline Hill.

When we reached the door of the Aurelian mansion, she turned and took the bundle from my arms. Her dark eyes met mine briefly, and the expression I read there left a bitter taste in my mouth.

Tears still rolling freely down her face, she returned to her quarters without a word, passing Agrippina on the way.

I chewed my lip, feeling uncomfortable. I did not know what to say or do, though in the pit of my stomach I knew what I had done was unkind. Swallowing down the guilt as I always did, I started for the kitchens.

I had not gone far when Agrippina grabbed my arm and spun me around. 'Look what thou hast done!' she exclaimed. 'I know thou carest not, but in spite of her kindness to thee, thou hast treated her cruelly. Thou shouldst be ashamed.' She swung her hand across my face and it met my cheek with a stinging *thwack*. Exhaling angrily, she stormed off to the kitchens, leaving me standing in the atrium.

Her words rang in my mind. *'Thou shouldst be ashamed.'* Why should I feel ashamed? The Romans had treated me with far more cruelty.

Then I stopped. I had no right to speak so to Aurelia. True, she was a Roman. But she was the only Roman who had been kind to me. Bitterness filled my mouth again and I slunk down to the kitchens, guilt and revenge warring in my heart.

I had behaved cruelly to Aurelia, and that could not be borne. I prided myself in the superiority of my people's culture, but this hypocritical act had revealed me to be no better than the ones who had taken away my freedom and hopes for the future.

I should have felt remorse and shame, but to my horror, I found that I did not. I felt only a murky apathy, and that frightened me terribly. Where would it end, this path of revenge?

CHAPTER VIII

I COULD NOT forget what Agrippina had said to me. Indeed, her words haunted me far into the evening when I went to Aurelia's chambers to freshen her up for *cena*.

I opened the door to her room without knocking and relit the lamps. She sat down silently on the only chair in the room and waited for me to finish. Then I undid her hair and combed my fingers through the silky strands, braiding it in the pattern she liked best. Until she was married, she could not put her hair up like the other wealthy ladies did.

Normally, Aurelia would have been chatting gaily about one thing or another, but this time she was silent. When I glanced at her face while putting the final touches on her hair, her eyes were swollen and there were traces of tears on her cheeks.

I felt another stab of guilt and looked away, ashamed of how cruelly I had repaid her kindness, yet too proud to bend and ask for forgiveness. I was Marcella now, an unfeeling slave; Enid, with all her sensitivities, was buried four years ago in the past. Enid, with her fearful fascination of the Redcrests, might have cared for Aurelia's feelings, but Marcella did not. To care and love opened one up to disappointment and pain, and I did not wish to suffer that pain again. I had shut myself up against the world and, refusing to love, set up a barrier that no one could break—a barrier behind which I was safe, though it was a cold, dull safety. In closing myself against the world and the past, I lost what love and happiness I could have found, even as a slave.

Aurelia left for the dining hall without a word to me and I, after preparing her room for when she would retire later that night, returned to the kitchens. Most of the slaves helped serve the meal, but as I was a personal slave, that requirement was not usually among my list of duties. I would aid in the preparation of the meal if I was needed or assist in the keeping of the house when it was required of me, but I mainly tended to Aurelia's wishes.

Down in the culina, some slaves scurried in and out while others completed the meal preparations. Agrippina gestured for me to help her stick bits of parsley around a roasted fowl. When we finished, I stepped back and licked my greasy fingers, tasting salt and fat. Agrippina wiped the sweat off her brow and turned to the large cauldron sitting over the fire to stir what would become our own supper. A stew, most likely. Stews and soups made using the remains of our master's meals was our usual fare, but I did not mind; Agrippina was skilled in making anything taste good.

She had been in the household most of her life, having acquired the skills from the previous cook to secure her own position. She trusted me more than she trusted the other slaves; I supposed it was because I was reliable and thorough, whereas the other slave women flirted and gossiped as much as they worked. Agrippina often bemoaned that fact, claiming it was because the Romans were becoming a decadent, irreverent society; she still prayed to the Greek gods and scoffed at the usage of their Roman names. That was one of very few things Agrippina kept from her childhood; in all else she had embraced her fate as a Roman slave without complaint.

As for me, my own gods had not rescued me from being sold as a slave, and I would rather have died than prostrated myself before a Roman idol. The Romans seemed to claim every culture's gods as their own—as well as everything else—renaming them to suit their fancy, as they had done with me.

I often watched the worship of the more superstitious slaves with bemused interest, forgetting that I had once been so myself. Whatever their names, the gods had never done anything good for me; therefore I prayed to none. Life had revealed to me that my people's gods were only figments of imagination. There was no more power in the oak tree than there was in a chunk of smooth marble.

'Marcella!'

I snapped out of my reverie. 'Aye, Agrippina?'

'Come, there is a moment's peace, Apollo be praised. Let us sup while we can.'

I nodded and helped clear off a portion of the large table in the kitchen, used mainly for preparing food. Unlike the luxurious Romans, we slaves did not recline at table, but sat or stood while eating. Agrippina placed simple wooden bowls on the table and ladled thick, steaming stew into them. Then she handed each of us who were standing there, some five in all, a piece of bread to eat with it.

I burned my tongue with the first bite and stuffed in a piece of bread to soothe my tingling mouth. It was good food, and I rarely got much of it as I was but one of many slaves.

Around me, my fellow slaves engaged in conversation with one another while those who were serving at table rushed in and out, refilling pitchers of wine and bearing platters heaped high with fowl, cheese, fruits, and bread. I supposed Aurelius must have many guests tonight, for they devoured far more than was usual for our master, his wife and daughter, and his two senator friends who often came to dine. At first, I was not listening to the conversation, as it did not concern me, but the sound of unfamiliar words caught my interest and I glanced up.

'Poor souls. Who would think they deserved such a fate?' one woman was saying.

'*Christiani*, that is what they are called. Who knew that they would be hated more than the Jews?' another put in.

A man spoke up this time. 'Yet one has to admire their bravery.'

'Stubborn, that is all they are,' Agrippina concluded. 'No one clings to their faith unto death, losing their life because of their beliefs. 'Tis foolishness.'

They continued to speak of it, but I was no longer paying heed; the slaves often spoke of criminals put to death in the newly-built Colosseum, heatedly discussing whether or not the punishment was just. Never having gone to the Games myself, I had little interest in them or those who died in them. I pitied the victims, for certainly some did not deserve it, but pity did no one much good, did it?

After I had finished eating, I placed my bowl into a large basin to be washed and I wiped my mouth on my hand, intending to escape for an hour while the master and his guests finished their meal.

'Marcella, stay here. I would have a word with thee.' Agrippina's voice had a tone that I dared not disobey. Finding a place in a corner from which to observe the comings and goings, I waited until she was free to speak with me. Then, 'Didst thou apologize to Aurelia for thy harsh words?'

I sighed softly, knowing where this question was leading. I shook my head in response, fidgeting where I stood.

Agrippina looked at me sadly, her hands on her hips. 'When wilt thou learn? Thou must apologize to her this very evening.'

'I cannot interrupt their dinner,' I argued.

'I should hope not! Marcella, use thine head. When thou preparest Aurelia for bed tonight, thou must apologize to her. Dost thou understand?'

I nodded again, knowing she would not let me go until I had agreed.

'Wilt swear it?'

'I swear,' I drawled, and departed.

Outside, the setting sun splashed rosy-gold light on the marble pillars of the peristylium. I leaned against one of them, feeling the cool stone through my thin tunic. I watched dully as the bubbling fountain continued to spew out shimmering water that caught the sun's dying colours and froze them into diamonds of glittering light.

The beauty was haunting.

For a brief moment, gazing at the crystal waters, I saw Telyn's face, his eyes flashing in the sunlight the same way the fountain did. The familiar ache of grief rose and I fought it down. I would not let the past rule me.

Shaking my head as if to somehow force the memories away, I retired to Aurelia's chambers to await her return. It was cold and I shivered. I did not know how long it would take for them to finish supping and, for all I knew, they could talk far into the night.

I was soon bored with simply waiting, and I began to look around the room for perhaps the thousandth time in my four years of slavery. Gazing at the objects lying on Aurelia's table, I noticed the silver-and-emerald necklace she had bought that morning.

Without realizing it, my hand strayed from where it hung at my side and my fingers brushed the cold gems. Then I seized it and clasped it around my neck, looking into the bronze mirror.

It clashed with my slave's tunic, but the emeralds matched my eyes. I nearly thought I was pretty—but then remembered it was no longer my place to adorn myself with such finery. Reluctantly, I unclasped the slender chain and laid it back down on the table.

'See, thou dost like pretty things.'

Aurelia's voice startled me and I jumped, whirling around to face her with wide eyes.

'Do not try to hide it. I know thou didst want it, even if 'twas only for a moment.' She stepped into the room and closed the door behind her.

'I was not going to steal it,' I mumbled, my ears burning.

'I did not say that. I said thou likest such things, even if thou dost continue to deny it.' She did not smile.

An awkward silence fell between us.

'I am sorry for what I said earlier,' I forced out, hating to humble myself and apologize. 'My words were cruel and thoughtless, and I should not have spoken them to thee. Wilt thou forgive me?' I continued to stare at the mosaics on the floor, following the pattern of intertwining vines.

'Aye, I forgive thee, Marcella. But why dost thou insist on the gap between us?'

My head whipped up. 'Aurelia, I am a slave. Even if thou shouldst free me, there would still be that strangeness between us. And even if thou didst forget I had been a slave, I would never forget. It will always lie between us.'

She chewed her bottom lip. 'But why?'

I sighed in frustration. 'I do not know how to make thee understand. Even'—I shrugged—'even if I had never been a slave, I am still a Briton. Our people are different. Like oil and water, Briton and Roman do not mix.'

'Is that because we enslaved thy people?'

I hesitated before answering. 'Aye, perhaps; yet not only that, but thy people slew our queen and her daughters and forced us to bow in submission to foreigners. Those are not things easily laid aside, especially between slave and master.'

'What is thy name?'

My heart stopped for a moment. 'M-my name?'

'Aye, thy Briton name.'

I opened my mouth, but no sound came out. Then I murmured, 'Marcella.'

Aurelia tightened her lips. 'That is thy Roman name.'

'Must thou take away my name as well?'

Another silence fell between us.

'Then do not tell me. I only wished to understand.' Aurelia spoke half-apologetically, but I knew she was displeased with me. She came closer and gestured for me to undo her hair and dress her for bed.

Having fulfilled my obligation towards her, I snuffed out the oil lamps and returned in the twilight to the kitchen. There, the peace of evening reigned. Agrippina sat by the fire, staring into the flames, her hands clasped in her lap.

My sandaled feet scuffled on the floor and she looked up.

'Didst thou apologize and make thy peace?'

Not exactly, I thought, but I only responded, 'Aye.'

'Good. Thou mayest go.'

I turned on my heel and departed, finding my way to the room where we women slept. Most were preparing to retire for the night, but I did not join their idle chatter. I pulled up the thin coverlet and closed my eyes, shutting out the world around me.

Just as the darkness of sleep began to swallow me up, Aurelia's words came back to me. I saw in my mind's eye her face framed by the lamplight, her lips pursed in thought. *It will always lie between us*, I had said. *But why?* was her response.

But why, indeed, I mused. *Why must there be a difference between Roman and Briton? Why can we not dwell together peacefully?*

Then I saw my father's face, caught by the flickering light of flames. *'They have stolen our lands, enslaved our people, murdered our queen, imposed their way of life upon us.... Will it never be enough for them? They accuse us of not submitting, but would they so easily submit were our places exchanged? I think not. They ask for peace, but it will not be so easily won as long as Roman blood remains upon this sacred ground...'*

Telyn appeared before me, his grey-eyed gaze sad and confused by my lack of understanding. *'Wouldst thou have us grovel before a people that needlessly dishonors and destroys our kind?*

Wouldst thou have us willingly surrender our freedom and all that is ours to a nation that seeks only to make us their bondservants? What dost thou not understand? Our ways and theirs are different; there can never be peace between us.'

Will peace ever be possible? Or will we always be kept apart?

I closed my eyes against the dark of the room and replaced it with the sheer black of my mind. It was impossible to think that Roman and Briton could ever love each other.

But then something came to mind—something I had nearly forgotten, something I had heard whispered by the elders of our village once—that Boudicca's daughter Brenyn had wed a Roman centurion out of love and had a son by him.

Perhaps it was possible, then. But not for me. I had lost too much.

CHAPTER IX

I OFTEN WONDERED whether Aurelia ever thought further on what had taken place between us. I know that I did. In the days that followed, my mind pored over and over again on the words that had passed between us, and I attempted time and again in vain to find an answer to her question: *But why?*

The next morning, Aurelia woke up as her usual bubbly self and I assumed she had forgotten the events of the night before. Neither she nor Agrippina spoke to me of it, not that any of the slaves had time for chatter.

Stepping down into the kitchens, I was nearly knocked over by a servant chasing a stray chicken across the floor. Glancing up, I sought an explanation from Agrippina, who, catching my gaze, shouted in response. Something along the lines of Aurelius' son returning on leave from the army and coming to dine tonight, and that we must prepare a feast worthy of him. I nodded in response and soon joined the few other bondwomen in plucking the feathers from the freshly-slain fowl.

Within moments, the kitchen was filled with the aromas of spices and burning wood, soon followed by the yeasty smell of bread and the mouth-watering scent of roasting meat. My stomach rumbled in response. I snatched up an apple and snuck off to the corner to devour it in peace, watching as cooks and servants simultaneously shouted orders at each other while preparing food for luncheon and dinner hours later.

The kitchens were always interesting around mealtimes, and today was no exception. Agrippina's hands and voice worked together in swift and perfect rhythm, and she just as skillfully smacked lazier slaves aside as she twisted bits of dough into complicated patterns. Another reason I often haunted these quarters was because there was always the possibility of free food to grab when no one was looking. I was a quiet worker and, although tall, slimmer than most of the other slaves, so I did not often get in other people's way. Few even noticed my presence save when Agrippina doted on me.

I suppose the only other explanation for why I spent most of my time in the kitchens was because all other work in the house was dull. I was no gardener, and I found dusting the library of Aurelius a monotonous chore, for collections of parchments and wax tablets with little black marks and indents had no value in my eyes.

'Marcella!'

I licked off the core of the apple one last time and tossed it into the pile of garbage to be taken out by lower ranking slaves. Rising to my feet, I reported to Agrippina.

'Marcella, I wouldst thou take those buckets and mop the atrium.'

I glanced behind me at the buckets and cloths and nodded. Gripping the handles tightly, I exited the premises and went to the atrium. The mosaics looked clean already, but I shrugged and knelt down, dipping the cloths in the warm water before wringing them out and wiping them across the artistic tiling.

I was grateful enough for the sunlight shining through the *compluvium*, the opening in the roof of the atrium, and reflecting off of the pool below, else I would have no light by which to see. It was odd enough that the villa of Aurelius did not have windows save on the second story, but when I had once asked about it, I had been laughed at and told it was the custom.

From time to time, papers rustled as Aurelius worked in his *tablinum*, and sometimes one could hear a faint crash followed by shouting from the culina if a careless slave left the door open, but that was all. Cold, rigid silence reigned. But I minded it little. I worked faster without the distraction of gossip.

Leaving the atrium with a thin layer of shiny, drying water, I returned to the kitchen and deposited the buckets there. Agrippina caught me in the act of escaping, and a moment later I found myself carrying platters of light lunch into the dining room where Aurelia and her mother were already reclining. I did not meet Aurelia's gaze and soon departed.

When luncheon was over, Aurelia and her mother went to lie down during the hottest hours of the day, as was their wont. As for me, I sought the rare opportunity to regain some lost sleep since Agrippina did not need me.

I soon regretted it.

A strange luminescence hung around me, as if the very air itself was light, shimmering and glowing with an ethereal radiance. I heard laughter and people speaking in my own tongue, the language I had not heard spoken by any save myself for four years. A few voices I recognized, but I could not see their faces.

Then I heard the notes of a harp and someone singing. It was Brynmor, his mellow voice upraised in some melancholy lament.

When the song ended, Ffionn's voice rang out, crying for something less dreary. Laughter followed.

Lilting notes answered him, a swift-moving song flowing from the harpist's fingers.

All at once, as suddenly as the sounds had come, they vanished and all was quiet....

I heard creaking and splashes and realized I was back on the ship bearing me towards Rome. All was dark and the ship pitched dreadfully as thunder echoed from above. The wind roared and then, again, the world was deathly still.

Telyn's voice whispered in my ear, 'Time is fleeting fast and soon everything will be changed. Do not forget us, Enid....'

I woke in a cold sweat, panting, my eyes racing around the room until I recollected my surroundings and my breathing quieted. Dropping my head in my hands, I closed my eyes and groaned.

Every time I was certain I had buried the past, it came back, more vivid and painful than before. Telyn's voice brought back a memory of the warmth I had always felt for him and the bitter injustice of my fate. Not only did it hurt, but it reminded me why I envied Aurelia. I envied her because she was young, beautiful, and free—everything I had once been and was no longer.

'Marcella?'

I looked up to see one of the bondwomen standing in the doorway. 'Aye?'

'Aurelia has awoken and is waiting for thee.'

I nodded and rose to my feet, pushing away the past.

That night, Aurelia returned to her chambers, speaking excitedly of her brother, Augustus. 'He has grown so much since last I saw him! Oh, Marcella, if thou hadst seen him before he joined the army, thou wouldst scarcely have recognized the scrawny lad he used to be.' She laughed, sitting down as I undid her hair. 'Now he is like the warriors in the tales and legends. And he knows so much! I doubt that any would stand a chance against him in combat!'

The corners of my mouth twitched in a smile as I remembered the vigorous training of my older brothers. While I had yet to meet this Augustus, I wondered if he was a match for Ffionn and Ilar. I had seen many soldiers of the Imperial Army patrolling the city and I thought that many of them would be easily beaten by a warrior of my own people. Had it not been for the disunity of the Celtic tribes, Rome would never have conquered Britannia.

Aurelia sighed as she climbed into her bed. 'I wish Augustus would bring one of his companions with him sometime. He keeps promising me, but never fulfilling it.'

'I am certain he will eventually,' I replied as I proceeded to extinguish the oil lamps. 'Good night, Mistress.'

'Good night, Marcella,' I heard her voice say sleepily as I closed the door behind me.

Returning to my own quarters, I lay down to sleep, but my eyes remained open. Around me, the other women turned in their sleep, breathing evenly. Though I made no sound, my soul moaned in silent agony, wishing to burst under the weight of endlessly suppressed grief—and yet it could not. Tears fell, but nothing else changed. The weight only grew greater.

I turned over, feeling utterly helpless and alone. I wondered if I could ever be free of it, this pain of longing for my past while knowing full well I could never return.

Then I remembered Telyn's words in my dream. What did he mean, *Soon everything will be changed…?* After four years of monotony, I would welcome a change, but I feared what it might be. In these uncertain days, masters were often murdered by one slave and the other slaves executed for the crime, despite their innocence. My mind raced, speculating about what Telyn could possibly have meant.

Twice my world had been turned upside down. The first time, it had been a year or two before my Roman captivity, during a celebration in the autumn. I had been helping my mother and the other women and girls serve by pouring the mead into the cups of the warriors gathered around a great fire. I was serving my brothers and their friends; Brynmor, of course, was shadowing Caradoc, and so was not among them. Upon hearing thanks, I looked up; my eyes met Telyn's crystal grey ones, shadowed by the firelight, as his smile lit up his face, and my heart had melted.

The second time had been my captivity and exile to Rome. I had lived as a slave in the household of Aurelius Augustus Trajan for four years now. I would have thought that after the shock of entering a new culture and the shame of my humiliation, nothing could move me, nothing could break me, nothing could melt away the hard ice that had locked itself around my heart.

They say things always come in threes; I could only hope that this third time would pay for all.

CHAPTER X

I T BEGAN WITH a whisper.

I caught a fragment of speech on my way to the kitchens and heard my name spoken by Aurelia. I froze, listening.

I did not recognize the male voices, though the inflection of one sounded similar to Aurelia's, and I fancied it to belong to her brother. The following words were imperceptible to me, so I continued on my way, brushing it off. Perhaps I had only imagined it after all.

It must have been midway through the evening meal when one of the slaves came into the kitchens bearing an empty platter and mumbled something about my presence being wanted in the dining room.

I glanced up in bewilderment at Agrippina, for I was never summoned to the dining room, but she merely shrugged.

Wiping my greasy and floured hands on my apron, I untied it and followed the slaves up to the dining room, my mind racing in an attempt to understand this sudden summons. Being taller than the others, I had a glimpse of the room before I was fully visible to the occupants who reclined at table.

The dining room was beautifully frescoed with scenes of the countryside outside of Rome. Gold leaf reflected the torchlight, making the room appear brighter than it was. Three low couches surrounded a large table, with space permitting slaves to easily place platters upon the table without leaning over their reclining masters.

The other slaves departed and I was left standing alone. I was acutely conscious that the eyes of all those seated at the table were fixed upon me, but I ignored them and looked only at Aurelia. I felt nervous and out of place; I did not belong here any more than they belonged in the kitchens.

Aurelia smiled when she caught sight of me and beckoned me closer. 'This is she of whom I spoke: Marcella.'

'But Marcella is a Roman name.' The voice that answered sounded much like Telyn's, only sweeter.

'Aye, but she yet refuses to tell me her British name.' Aurelia laughed and raised her goblet of wine to her lips.

I scarcely heard her reply. I was staring at the young man who had spoken. I had seen him before, but I could not remember where. Like most Romans, he boasted blue-black hair and smooth olive skin, but he lacked the hooked nose—his was straight and slender like those of the Greeks. Yet it was his eyes that caught my attention. They were neither the glimmering pools of darkness nor the misty grey of most Romans, but a glowing olive-gold that flashed in the torchlight. His gaze met mine and held it until I looked away, feeling a blush spread across my face.

I knew now where I had seen him. It was he who had grabbed my arm when I attempted to run away four years ago, the day I had been so close to freedom—and Telyn. But the young soldier made no sign of recognition; I hoped he had forgotten.

'Perhaps thou shouldst tell her why thou sent for her,' the young man prompted.

'I agree. Aurelia, why didst thou?' Honoria said more sternly.

Aurelia tittered nervously. 'When Augustus mentioned that Lucius was of British blood, I thought to bring Marcella in, since she is from Britannia.'

I looked at the youth again, my wonder growing. I was almost overwhelmed seeing someone who was, in a way, from my own homeland. Now that I knew, I could sense something unmistakably Celtic about him—he even appeared less Roman to me than at first. Perhaps his British blood was why he looked so much like Telyn.

'Marcella is from Britannia?' Lucius questioned with interest, setting down his glass with a distinct click on the table.

'Aye, she was brought here a few years ago and has been my slave ever since.'

Lucius glanced from Aurelia to me, and then back again. I now saw the recognition in his eyes; he remembered our meeting in the street so long ago. 'Dost thou mind if I ask her a few questions?'

Aurelia shrugged and smiled. 'I mind not.'

I heard Honoria clear her throat with obvious disapproval, but no one noticed her.

'Marcella—'

I looked at Lucius and tried my utmost to remain still. He spoke gently, as if treading on glass, afraid of shattering it, and yet there was a pulsing eagerness in the undertone of his question.

'From what tribe dost thou hail?'

The blood rushed from my face. My mouth was suddenly dry, and I forced my answer out in a hoarse whisper. 'From the Iceni.'

I heard gasps from around the table and his eyes widened in surprise—surprise and something else I could not lay a finger on. Since Boudicca's rebellion, a few years before my birth, that particular British tribe had maintained a peculiar place of interest in Roman society. After all, it was an uncommon woman who could almost succeed in overthrowing the Empire's rule.

'Didst thou not say thy mother was Iceni?' Augustus spoke now through a mouthful of roasted chicken.

Lucius looked down and cleared his throat. His face was flushed. 'Aye. She was the elder daughter of Boudicca.'

My mouth must have dropped open in shock, for I mind closing it slowly without any remembrance of why I had to do so. 'Truly?'

'Aye.' He gazed up at me and we stared at each other for a long moment, this new knowledge somehow changing everything. Then Lucius said softly, '*Mae'n ddrwg gennyf glywed am eich colled. Ni ddylai unrhyw un erioed fod yn gaethweision rhywun arall.*'

'W-what did he say?' Aurelia rose up on one elbow, gaping at the pair of us watching each other.

'I said, "I am sorry to hear of thy loss. No freeborn person should ever be another's slave,"' Lucius translated, his eyes never leaving mine.

'*Diolch. Chi yw'r cyntaf i gydymdeimlo,*' I replied just as softly. It was odd and refreshing to hear and speak my native tongue— odd because it had been four years since last I spoke it aloud, refreshing because it was a part of me that had long been buried. And that Lucius was speaking it to me—not translating the Latin tongue, but speaking like a native—was almost more than I could bear. I wanted to cry for the sheer joy of it, and yet I could not. None of those watching us would understand.

'And what did Marcella say back?' Honoria's voice had an edge of warning and I knew I was very close to being punished for possibly hinting at rebellion.

'She said, "Thank you. Thou art the first to care."' A hint of a smile twitched at the corners of Lucius' mouth and I felt encouraged and warmed by his lack of animosity. Something in him bonded us in that moment—perhaps his British ancestry—and I wanted to know him as a person and a friend rather than a Roman and an enemy.

'I think this has gone on long enough. Marcella, thou art dismissed,' Aurelius broke in, and the moment was shattered.

I bowed my head and left the room, my mind whirling. I scarcely saw the way back to the kitchens and felt my way down the stairs, ignoring the questions thrown at me by the other servants, including Agrippina. When she realized I was wrapped up in my own thoughts, she merely sighed and shook her head.

Mechanically, I chopped away at the small heap of vegetables Agrippina gave me, but my thoughts were elsewhere.

Lucius, a British Roman. Was such a thing even possible? Could it even be believed? A Roman of mixed descent—and not only that, but of Boudicca's blood. Why then, he was of my own people!

The whole idea was so alien to me that I knew not what to do with it. This occurrence and my dream of Telyn could not be mere coincidence, could they? Was someone trying to tell me something? And if so, then who? Was there such a thing as Fate, that some say governs the lives of men, or were there indeed gods controlling the universe?

These questions continued to repeat themselves in my mind when I went to Aurelia's chambers to prepare her for bed that night.

'What didst thou think of Lucius?' came her first inquiry as I entered.

'What am I supposed to think of him?' I was bewildered by her words and by the whole encounter with Lucius, along with the entangled musings that had arisen from it.

'Well, he is British; of the same tribe as thee, it appears.'

I sighed softly. 'Aye, he is.'

She shook her pretty head and stated, 'I think him quite handsome, dost thou not?'

'I think one of my station is not permitted to think such things,' I responded dryly.

'Oh, Marcella!' Aurelia turned around, her hair, half undone, slipping out of my hands. 'Dost thou never dream?'

I stared at her, my thoughts racing after each other too fast to be spoken. *Of course, I dream. I dream, and I hate to dream. I hate to dream, for I know that it will never be so. Dream away—thou canst afford it, but I have no hope. 'Tis better not to dream at all than to dream with no hope of having.*

Her eyes went wide in fear. 'Marcella, why dost thou look at me like that?'

I checked, my heart skipping a beat. 'Like what?' I tried to remain calm as I reached forward to take up her half-unbraided hair, but my hands trembled slightly at the raw emotion that had stormed its way into my soul. Rarely did such passions seize me; they frightened me, if anything did, for I did not want to be punished for what others might take as rebellion. Besides, it was easier to live life unfeeling than to suffer for it.

'Thou lookest as if I had stabbed thee. I only asked if thou dost ever imagine such things as—' A blush rosied her cheeks and she did not continue, but I knew what she meant.

'I did, once, but that was long ago.' I spoke softly and guardedly, not trusting myself to say more.

To my relief, she flew onto another subject. 'I think it is terrible that those in the army cannot wed until they are old. 'Tis such a pity.'

'They can wed,' I replied promptly, 'but not in the eyes of Roman law.'

Aurelia sighed. 'Father would never permit it, anyway.'

'I think Lucius would also have to return thy affections,' I dared to add, 'but he and thou have only just met.'

Her lips turned downward into a pout. 'Marcella, thou art no fun.'

She said no more, but once or twice in the mirror I caught a mischievous glimmer in her eyes.

The next day, in the kitchens, I found myself subject to every bit of imaginable gossip. The girls tittered among themselves, and soon I caught whispers that told me all I needed to know. Agrippina once gave me a questioning look, but I said nothing about it until an incident occurred after the midday meal had been served.

As the servant girls were bringing back the small remnants of uneaten food, Agrippina demanded to know of what they were speaking endlessly.

One of them giggled and replied, 'Why, didst thou not hear of what happened last night?'

My face flushed hot.

'I remember nothing out of the ordinary happening, save that Marcella was called up to the dining room,' Agrippina replied nonchalantly, as if such a thing happened all the time.

'Aye, at the request of Aurelia.' Another laugh followed that statement and I snorted in disgust.

'Well, thou might as well tell me the whole matter.' Agrippina was as frustrated as I was, though, I think, for a different reason.

'Aurelia wished to show Marcella off to a young soldier friend of Augustus', whose mother was of the same tribe of barbarian Britons as Marcella.' More giggling followed.

'I see,' Agrippina concluded, casting me a glance as if to say we would talk about it later, but her attempt to end the conversation was futile.

'After both boys left,' the girl continued, 'Aurelius said he was ashamed of his daughter's behaviour in bringing in a mere slave during their dinner. He also said he wished to hear no more talk of his son associating'—the girl blushed and snickered— 'with a British *bastard*.'

'Enough! I will hear no such profanity in my kitchen, especially not from the likes of thee!' Agrippina fairly chased the girl out, righteous indignation on her face. Then she turned and faced the rest of the servants assembled in the room. 'I wish to hear no such language in this place. And no more degradation of Marcella's heritage. She is no lower a slave than any of ye here.' With another huff for emphasis, she sent them all out and instructed me to tidy the dining room, muttering something about me being the only dependable servant left.

The *triclinium* was mostly clean, but I did not argue with Agrippina. 'Twas not wise to do so, not when she was in such a rage. I cleaned and mopped the room as swiftly as I could, trying to push the scene from the night before out of my mind, but it was nearly impossible.

Every time I glanced up, I saw the torchlight illuminating Lucius' green-gold eyes and heard his voice—so much like Telyn's—in my mind. It haunted me, and for that I was afraid of him, almost to the point of hatred. 'Twas hard enough to bury the past only for it to resurface in my sleep; it was quite another matter to have it materialize before my eyes in broad daylight. And yet I could not hate him, even if I feared that in the end he would be no different from any other Roman.

'Marcella! Aurelia requests thy presence immediately!' A voice broke into my musings and I looked up, bewildered.

'Whatever for?' I retorted none too kindly.

The bondwoman shrugged. 'She said it was a matter of utmost importance and secrecy.'

I rose to my feet and picked up the bucket of sudsy water, depositing it into the hands of my fellow slave. I was finished anyway.

When I reached Aurelia's chambers, she turned around and faced me, the same strange gleam in her eyes that I had seen the night before. She hurriedly beckoned me to close the door behind me. 'Quick!' she exclaimed. 'We must make haste!'

CHAPTER XI

AURELIA, WHATEVER CANST thou mean?' I demanded breathlessly.

She cast a coy smile over her shoulder. 'What dost thou think?' She continued to rummage through a small collection of belongings she had spread out on her bed.

I shrugged helplessly. 'What am I supposed to think? Thou summonest me here and sayest we are going out. Then thou sayest I must tell no one of what we are doing and that it is part of some great secret. And yet all the while thou sayest nothing as to what—*exactly*—we are going to do.'

She laughed and straightened. 'Well then, if only thou wilt brook no argument and do exactly as I say.'

I raised a sceptical eyebrow.

'Oh, come, Marcella! 'Tis no harm—save that Mater would have a fit if she knew. Thou knowest how much she despises me going out without a male attendant unless it be to the Forum after the baths.'

'Then why canst thou not take someone better suited?'

Aurelia sat down on her bed beside her paraphernalia and huffed. 'Because it is thee that I need.'

I squinted in bewilderment. 'What? Why?'

She threw her hands into the air. 'We are going to pay a visit to someone on the Caelian Hill.'

'That is a far distance. 'Twill take at least half of an hour to get there—should nothing bar our way.'

She shrugged. 'And?'

'Who, precisely, are we going to visit? Is it someone thy family knows?'

'We are going to visit Julia Maxima. Mater used to visit her often when I was very little.'

'Who is that?' Despite my attempts to retain a nonchalant tone, I feared my voice took on an edge of uneasiness. What was Aurelia getting me into?

She smiled, that strange twinkle once again appearing in her eye. 'Why, she is Lucius' grandmother. And the only surviving member of his family besides his cousin.'

'But why would we visit her?'

'I wish to know more about this young Lucius, even if thou dost not. Besides, I have not seen her in ages.'

I suppressed the urge to groan. 'Aurelia, thou saidst thyself last night thou couldst never marry him according to Roman law.'

'Aye, that is so. However, that rule does not apply to every-one, thyself included. And I am going to visit her, and thou'—she placed an assortment of items in my hands—'art going with me as a friend.'

'Aurelia, thou art mad. She would see through the disguise at once. Nothing thou canst do will ever persuade anyone that I am a Roman. I cannot even speak the Latin tongue without an accent.'

My mistress only smiled triumphantly at me. 'That is why thou art going as my companion, who was raised in Britannia, and is here with her father who is one of many scholars in Londinium.'

'This is foolishness,' I replied stubbornly.

'Oh, Marcella, please? For my sake?'

'If we are caught, I will not take the blame.'

'Agreed. Thou art coming with me, then?'

'It appears I have no other choice.'

'Ah, good.' Aurelia began returning unneeded accessories to the great chest where she kept them. Then she turned to me and said, 'Let me dress thee.'

Helplessly, I stripped off my slave's tunic and stepped into the soft *toga praetexta*, feeling as guilty as if I were committing a crime. Such rich garments belonged to the Enid of four years past, not to the slave Marcella.

Aurelia looked me over and nodded, clicking her tongue much like Agrippina did when she approved of something. 'Now, sit thyself down.'

'Might it not be best if I braid my own hair?' I ventured. I doubted Aurelia had ever arranged hair, since she always had servants to do it for her.

'Well, canst thou do it thyself?' She wrinkled her nose in disbelief.

'Perhaps not as well as thine, but it will serve its purpose.' I undid the braids that were wound about my head and held in place with wooden pins. Running my fingers through the flame-coloured strands, I gazed at my reflection in the mirror, wooden pins held in between my teeth, as I tried to recreate the same pattern I wove in Aurelia's hair every day. It was nowhere as neat as hers, but it would do. I used the pins to stick the loose strands into place and then turned to my mistress for inspection.

She shrugged. 'It will do, I suppose. Now, I have just the *stola* for thee.' Producing an emerald-coloured garment, she held it up for me to see.

'That is too fine, even for a disguise. What if thy mother sees me?'

Aurelia laughed. 'Do not be so terrified. I shall claim full responsibility. Besides, Mater is out visiting with friends. She will not be back until this evening and *Pater* never pays attention to me anyway. Put it on—I wish to see how it matches the colour of thy eyes.'

The light, flowy folds of the material settled around me as Aurelia pinned the sleeves together on my shoulders with gold pins. It felt so soft and genteel; seeming both right and wrong to wear it. Right, because such clothing was worthy of any chieftain's daughter in Britannia, but at the same time dreadfully wrong because I was a slave. It was no longer my place to wear such finery, even if it did look well on me.

'There, I think it suits thee. Now, if only....' She shook her head. 'Perhaps some other time. Meanwhile, thou canst wear this.' She held up the emerald-and-silver necklace she had purchased only a few days before and clasped it around my neck before I could protest.

For a split second, my slave façade fell to pieces. I remembered when I had briefly worn that very necklace, how it had matched my eyes so perfectly, how in that half-breath of a moment I had wanted to wear it—to enjoy pretty things again as I had before I was enslaved. But the moment passed and the guilt and wrongness of it all settled back on my shoulders. 'Aurelia, I must not—!'

'I will not pay heed to a word thou sayest. Come, we must be going.' She seized my hand and dragged me out of her room, across the peristylium, and through the passageway that ran past her father's tablinum. I glanced at the hangings that separated the two rooms, feeling my heart thudding in my chest, but Aurelia only continued through the atrium and out the gates of the villa.

Without another word, she led me swiftly through the crowded streets of Rome. I avoided the looks of passersby as we crossed the distance between the Esquiline and Caelian hills. I felt guilt rather than pride in my fine clothes and jewels. We skirted the massive Colosseum and passed the towering living places of the poorer classes, stepping quickly to avoid waste being dumped on our heads. Aurelia still clutched my hand, as if she was afraid I would run back to the villa if she let go.

I was trembling all over, terrified that someone would see through my disguise and accuse me of climbing above my station. It was a foolish fear, for who would recognize me among the other million inhabitants of the Eternal City? But it haunted me all the same as we climbed the gently sloping rise of the Caelian hill.

At last, Aurelia slowed our quick pace, looking at the gates of each house carefully. Finding the one she wanted, she turned to me with another smile and led me through the gates and up to the double wooden doors that marked the entrance to the Septimius villa.

She knocked and waited for a response.

My heart pounded in my throat. *Suppose this Julia suspects our ruse? Suppose she is not at home at all? Suppose we come back late and Honoria sees us?*

The door opened to reveal a portly steward with a balding head. 'Who art thou?' He squinted at us down his thin nose.

'I am Aurelia, daughter to Aurelius Augustus Trajan, the senator, on visit to Mistress Julia Laelia Maxima. With me is my companion, Marcella.'

I felt the blood drain away from my face. *She did not even bother to change my name?*

The steward squeaked through his nose. 'Ah, come in then, come in. The mistress is in the peristylium. Right this way, if thou pleasest.'

If I had thought the Aurelian mansion grand, this one was far superior. Unlike many Roman villas, it had windows on the ground floor. The bright sunlight glittered off of the gold leaf that tinted the walls and marble columns in the atrium—an atrium that had the customary benches around the walls but seemed to be missing something I could not place. The gardens were kept in a neater pattern than those at the Aurelian villa, but the peristylium was much the same as the one I knew well.

We found Julia seated on a marble bench beside a flowering rhododendron bush, studying a papyrus scroll. She was robed in a saffron *stola* with gold embroidery on the hem, and jeweled combs were set in her golden hair, hair marked with strands of white. She looked up at us as we entered and she smiled—a pleasant smile, but accompanied by confusion in her pale grey eyes.

'Mistress, these two *filias* are here to see thee.' The steward cleared his throat awkwardly.

Before Julia could respond, the sound of footsteps was heard and a lithe, wiry figure appeared among the columns. He stepped into the sunlight and I felt my heart leap into my throat for fear.

Lucius caught sight of us and his lips parted in surprise. 'Why, Aurelia, thou didst not tell me thou would visit. And why is—?'

'My companion with me?' Aurelia interrupted him, a pleasant smile on her face.

I looked at the ground, my face burning with embarrassment.

'I wished her to come,' she explained with the same ease as she might comment on the beauty of the rhododendron blossoms.

'Ah, I see....' His voice trailed off.

I glanced up and he nodded towards me, a slight dip of his dark head, but I took it to mean that he understood the whole predicament.

'Lucius, how dost thou know them?' Julia turned towards her grandson. 'Thou didst never tell me that Augustus was of the Aurelian family.'

'I only met them last night, when Augustus took me to his father's villa on the Esquiline.'

'Lucius!' Another male voice broke in and we turned as one to face yet another young man entering the peristylium.

I heard Aurelia draw in her breath sharply. She stared at the newcomer, her lips parted in wonder.

I glanced back at the young man. He was tall with a muscular build and he shared similar facial features as Lucius, only he had his grandmother's grey eyes and a nose that reminded me of a falcon.

'Lucius, who are these people?' He drew his thick, dark brows together in pleasant surprise.

'They are friends, Rufus. The sister of Augustus and her—erm—companion.'

Rufus turned towards us. ''Tis a pleasure to make the acquaintance of such lovely young women.' He smiled and bowed, but I noted with amusement that he looked only at Aurelia.

'Lucius'—Julia rose from her seat—'didst thou invite them here?'

'Nay, but I came of my own accord,' Aurelia responded boldly. 'I did not know he would be here at all. 'Twas thee I came to see. It has been long since Mater visited thee, methinks.'

'Ah, I see.' Julia smiled warmly at Aurelia, recognition in her eyes, but she appeared unsure where I was concerned. For my part, I fought the urge to scuffle my feet and run.

'Lady Aurelia, dost thou have an interest in books?' Rufus questioned.

'Why, of course!'

I knew she was lying, yet I said nothing. She had no more interest in books than I did, but I supposed she wished to spend time in the company of this handsome youth.

'Well then, dost thou wish to see our library?' He offered her his hand with a smile.

Aurelia beamed back and took it, leaving the four of us alone—three, once Julia nodded to the steward to depart.

Lucius stepped forward until he stood beside me. 'Marcella, what is the meaning of all this?' He spoke to me in a low tone, but Julia noticed it all the same.

'It was Aurelia; she made me come.'

'Lucius, who is this young lady?'

I glanced nervously at Lucius, but he said nothing. Fear weighed heavily on me. What would Julia say if she discovered I was only a slave? 'I—I am Marcella.'

'Thou dost not look Roman.' It was more of a question than an answer.

I kept my eyes on the red, white, and yellow mosaic pattern on the floor as my heart began to pound again and my face flushed red. I felt Lucius' fingers gently brush against my own and my heart skipped a beat, a strangely familiar warmth tingling in my hands. Had not Telyn done the same thing once?

'Marcella is from Britannia; she shares similar heritage to me,' Lucius said calmly.

'Ah, but Marcella is not a British name, Lucius. Thou and I both know that.'

'She has not yet told me her British name.'

'And why would that be?' Julia rose from the bench, the parchment springing together in her hands. Despite her controlled voice, there was an apprehensive look in her eyes that made me wonder what she could possibly fear from me.

'*Avia*, I met her only last night. Unlike most *filias*, she is not one to freely speak. And I believe she has a choice whether to reveal to a complete stranger such as I her British name.' His tone was heated.

'Nay, Lucius, that is not what I asked,' Julia replied gently. 'I asked why, being from Britannia, she would have a *Roman* name along with her British one.'

Her eyes bored into me as if she could see right through the disguise. Lucius opened his mouth and closed it again, clenching his jaw. I could keep silent no longer—so much for Aurelia's lies.

'Mistress Julia, perhaps 'twould be better if I answer thine uncertainties myself. 'Tis true, I am from Britannia and have no Roman blood in my veins. I am of the same tribe as Lucius' mother, but was captured and sold as a slave to Aurelia some four years ago. She brought me with her to thy villa this after-noon in the guise of a companion because she wished to speak with thee on some matter in which she had interest.'

I watched Julia's face carefully, but her expression was blank. 'I see.' She looked me up and down, and I writhed inwardly at her penetrating gaze. 'Marcella, my grandson Lucius has often been scorned by society because of his heritage. Not only is he of British blood, but he is illegitimate, though heir to my second child and only son, Justus Julius Septimius. Lucius' great-uncle led the legions that put down Boudicca's rebellion and therefore loathes the sight of him and speaks ill of him in the company of his superiors. But I never hated him. Nor do I despise any Briton, be they slave or free. If thou art trusted by Lucius, then thou art always welcomed here.' She smiled now, a warm smile, but a small lump of unease remained in my throat. I did not trust any Roman easily—even if they were kind to me. I did not want to be hurt again.

We heard laughter coming down the corridor—Aurelia and Rufus were returning. Julia traced a rough outline of a fish in the dirt with her sandaled foot, looking intently at her grandson. I did not understand and glanced up at Lucius, who only shook his head at her. She brushed over it and the image vanished, still mysterious to me as ever.

'We had such a marvelous time, did we not, Aurelia?' Rufus smiled at the girl at his side, never having noticed. 'A pity thou canst not stay longer.'

'Oh yes! Marcella, even thou might have enjoyed it!' She giggled lightly.

'Shall we have them again, *Avia*?' Rufus asked eagerly.

Julia smiled. 'Perhaps, perhaps we shall. But we must not keep them. Already the sun is sinking.'

Aurelia laughed some sort of goodbye to Rufus.

I turned away, as if to leave immediately, but a gentle voice stopped me. 'Farewell until we meet again, Marcella.'

My gaze flickered upwards and met Lucius', the intensity of the setting sun striking his copper eyes so they glowed like molten gold. There was a timid smile on his lips and a look of pity in his glance.

'Farewell,' I responded, my voice sounding cold and emotionless in my own ears.

'Come, Marcella, we must make haste,' Aurelia called, and I hastened to join her as we exited the Septimius villa.

We ran nearly all the way back to the Esquiline Hill, my heart thudding in my throat, hoping against hope that Honoria would not have returned yet.

Breathlessly, we entered and dashed through the corridor, the hangings of the tablinum fluttering as we rushed past, slamming the door to Aurelia's chamber closed. Then we leaned against the wall, trying to catch our breath.

'Well, we made it,' Aurelia gasped.

'Aye, we did.' I stumbled forward and took off the necklace, quickly changing into my slave garments and leaving the finer clothes on Aurelia's bed. I would return them to their proper place at another time.

'Where art thou going?'

'Agrippina will be wanting to know my whereabouts.'

'What wilt thou tell her?'

'That thou required me on some errand.'

Aurelia nodded. 'I will call thee when the hour for dinner draws near.'

I left and made my way across the slowly darkening peristylium to the kitchens. Yet even as I descended the small stair, Lucius' face came before my eyes, the light striking his handsome features with intensity as he said farewell. I tightened my jaw, trying to remember Telyn's face.

But despite how hard I tried, I only saw Lucius.

CHAPTER XII

'WHAT DIDST THOU think of Rufus?' Aurelia questioned me that evening as I prepared her for bed.

I looked up to meet her gaze in the mirror as I combed my fingers through her hair one last time. 'Why dost thou ask?'

'Out of curiosity, of course. Why else would I ask?'

I shrugged and pulled back the covers of her bed. 'I have not spent enough time in his company to form an opinion of him.'

'Fair enough.' She climbed into bed and pulled the bedclothes over her as I turned to snuff out the lights. 'Marcella, dost thou fancy Lucius?'

I wheeled around defensively. 'Of course not! I have scarcely seen him for more than a day. I would not care for him even if it was not beyond my station.'

'Why not? He seems pleasant enough.'

I sighed. 'I barely know him enough to speak to, let alone to fancy him in any way. Sleep well, Mistress.' I left the room, closing the door softly behind me.

That night, I dreamt of home—and yet it was not my home. The people were the same, the village was the same, but it was all distant and unreal, as if I were only a spectator watching them all behind a glassy wall. I heard their voices and called out to them, but they could not hear me.

Then I heard Telyn's voice, calling my name in excitement. *'Enid! Enid!'*

But when I turned to look at him, I saw Lucius....

I woke the next morning in confusion. I remembered Telyn's words, *Time is fleeting fast, and soon everything will be changed. Do not forget us, Enid....*

How could I ever forget them? But what did it all mean? Did he speak of Lucius, or something else entirely?

These questions echoed in my mind all through the morning so that I scarcely focused on anything else. Even Aurelia gave me a strange look when I accompanied her to the baths.

When I returned at last to the Aurelian mansion, I retired to the kitchens and found them quiet. Most of the servants were resting in the heat of the day, and only Agrippina sat in a chair in a corner, dozing lightly.

I snatched one of the apples on the counter and sat in my hiding place in the kitchens, gnawing hungrily until I reached the core and sucked the remaining juices out. Unfortunately, it made quite a bit of noise and Agrippina awoke, staring around the room in sleepy terror to find the source of the noise.

'Marcella, is it thee?'

'Aye,' I replied, tossing the apple core into the small pile of vegetable refuse waiting to be thrown out.

'What has happened to thee? Thou hast been in a strange mood these last few days.'

I knew she meant it kindly, but I had no desire at the moment to be asked questions I could not even answer myself. 'Nothing of importance,' I responded after a moment of silence.

'Art thou speaking the truth?'

'If I wished thee to know, I would have told thee.' My tone was regrettably harsh.

Agrippina looked at me, pity in her eyes, and pursed her lips. 'Marcella, thine heart will never heal if thou dost shun people always. Like a plant hidden in darkness, it will not grow and thrive if it never sees the light again.'

'And if I do not wish to grow and thrive?' A foolish question, but I asked it all the same.

'And why wouldst thou not? Thou hast a good master and a kind mistress. Thou art cared for under this roof. Thou art kept safe from the host of horrible evils that lurk outside the walls of this villa. There is no reason thou shouldst not wish to live life as best as thou can.'

'There is a reason,' I answered at last. 'Those things may be true, but they do not lighten the yoke of slavery, nor do they soothe my longing for my own people and my own home. Even should I be freed, I would still be an outcast. I am a Briton, a barbarian in the eyes of these people. I know no one, and how would I ever return to my home?'

Agrippina rose to her feet and stretched. 'Then that is thine own choice. I can only hope thou wilt not grow to regret it.' She turned and began preparing food for the evening meal several hours hence, and I supposed that my presence was no longer wanted. So I left.

Aurelia had still not returned, so I stood in the shadows of the peristylium, leaning my face against one of the cool columns, watching the slanting rays of the sun slowly travel across the garden. It was during times like these that I often stared at nothing, concentrated on nothing. It was sort of like blanking my mind to all else; it was the only way I could live as an obedient, submissive, and unintelligent slave for the last four years.

I had always loved knowledge; I would often shadow the elders' places during feasts and councils, if I could attend them, and listen to their discussions. It was the only way I learned about the world beyond our hills and valleys. We rarely talked about the Redcrests, and when they were spoken of, it was in dark whispers voiced around the dying embers of a fire. I listened with wide eyes, drinking in the knowledge of the forbidden. Little had I known that I would one day rue that intense interest.

Lucius' face came to mind and I closed my eyes, trying to shut him out and bring back the memory of Telyn. I endeavoured to hear his mellow voice, the pleasant ring that sent thrills through my being. But it was futile.

'Oh, Telyn!' I whispered into the peaceful silence. 'Why art thou so far from me?'

And for once, I dared to think of home.

I wondered how my family was—whether Ffionn and Ilar had been betrothed and married yet, whether any of my sisters were wedded, whether Brynmor had found something besides music to love—and Telyn. Was he betrothed or wedded to someone else yet? And if so, to whom? Or did he believe I was still alive and was patiently waiting for me?

But no. They probably all thought me dead and had given up hope that I would ever return. I had given up long ago.

An opening and closing of doors startled me, and I realized I had been crying. Wiping my face to remove the telltale signs of tears, I went to Aurelia's chamber—she would surely call upon me in a moment.

'Ah, Marcella,' my mistress said as I entered. 'I had the most wonderful time.'

'Where didst thou go?' I replied out of habit.

'Oh, to Alexandria's villa. She wished me to come and spend time with her and her other companions. Thou knowest she is to be married?'

'Nay,' I replied, my fingers deftly fixing her hair in preparation for supper that evening.

Aurelia sighed. 'I wish I was to be married.'

'Dost thou have anyone in mind?'

'Well, Rufus is quite handsome.'

'Is he free?' I found it hard to picture Aurelia as the matron of a wealthy Roman household, let alone wife to a man like Rufus. She still seemed so young to me.

'Oh, quite so. He wishes to become a scholar, or perhaps a senator—maybe even a consul someday. That would please Pater. Besides, it is a good match.'

I said nothing, only applied the finishing touches to her hair.

'And thee, wilt thou ever fancy someone?' She turned around to face me. 'Or wilt thou forever be cold and heartless?'

I froze, feeling a surge of hurt coursing through my veins. She was probing me too deeply for comfort.

'I have no other choice,' I forced out at last.

'No other choice? Why, Marcella, it is not natural!'

'I am a freeborn slave! Is that natural?' I snapped. Without waiting for a reply, I left the room and hastened to the kitchens.

Agrippina did not question my stormy expression as I entered, for which I was grateful. I had no desire to engage in conversation with anyone at that moment. Anger burned in my heart and at such times I was liable to lash out without warning.

I did not speak another word that evening and retired for the night, feeling an aching emptiness in my heart. It did not vanish away in the morning and persisted throughout the day.

I dreaded paying another visit to Julia that afternoon. I would have done anything to avoid being in Lucius' presence again. I knew he meant only kindness to me, but Telyn was drifting farther and farther away. I was losing the only memory I allowed myself to indulge in, and it terrified me. What if I forgot my people, my homeland, all that was so dear to me still?

That afternoon, Julia answered Aurelia's knock herself and greeted us with a smile. She led us through the atrium and out into the grey humidity of the peristylium. The sun was hidden behind a thick veil of clouds, but the heat was still oppressive.

This time, I was clothed only in my slave's tunic. It was cooler than the fine garments I had worn last time, but, for the first time in my four years of slavehood, I felt ashamed of it. It was a constant reminder of my slavery, and some part of me wanted Julia to see me as Lucius did—as an equal human being. A stab of envy shot through me as I looked at Aurelia, and I turned away. Envy helped no one.

'Is Rufus here?' I heard Aurelia say.

Julia smiled. 'Aye, I am sure he will be here soon. Meanwhile, thou art welcome to sit down.' She called for her steward, and he brought three cups of *mulsum,* a drink of wine and honey.

I could scarcely drink and my hands trembled. My throat struggled to swallow, but I forced down a polite amount so as not to appear rude. All the while I waited in anxiety, listening for Lucius' footsteps. Was he here or was he at the military barracks? I wanted to ask Julia, but I did not wish to show an undue interest in her grandson.

A moment later, Rufus appeared through the columns of the peristylium and smiled a greeting to the three of us. Aurelia rose at once and followed him away, the pair of them laughing and talking. They left us in silence and I tried again to drink, if only to appear occupied.

'Marcella, how dost thou fare?' Julia asked gently.

'Well enough,' I lied. 'And thee?'

'Life is good.' She smiled encouragingly. 'Does Aurelia treat thee well?'

'I suppose.' I shrugged. 'But slavery is a bitter thing,' I dared to add a moment later, hardly knowing why I said it.

''Tis better to be treated kindly than cruelly. For then the bitterness would be worse.'

I nodded after a minute's reflection. 'Perhaps so.'

'Is there naught of interest for thee in thy free moments?'

'Nay, why should there be?' I was confused as to why she would ask such a thing. Why did Julia care so much about the happiness of a slave?

Julia took a swallow of her drink. 'Dost thou enjoy reading?'

I looked at her blankly. 'I do not know how to read.'

'Forgive me. I should have known that being British and a female-slave, thou wouldst not have learnt such a thing.... But wouldst thou like to?'

'How?' How indeed. Aurelia would never teach me, nor would anyone else in the household of Aurelius.

'I could teach thee. I am thinking Aurelia may wish to visit often.' A youthful light twinkled in her eyes. 'It will keep the hours from becoming tedious.'

'But why shouldst thou want me to learn?'

Julia looked straight into my eyes. 'Marcella, I only wish to be kind to thee. I will not make thee learn if thou dost not wish it.'

'I would, very much, but I feared there was some dark design behind it all.'

Julia laughed, a pleasant sound, and I felt my face redden.

'May I ask thee a question?' I ventured, suddenly remembering something I had noticed both times I had walked through her atrium.

'Of course. What is it?'

'I noticed the first time we came here that thou dost not have a shrine to Laertes and the other household gods that most Romans keep. Dost thou not worship them as they do?'

I instantly regretted my words, for Julia paled drastically—I nearly thought she would swoon.

A moment later, though, she assumed her natural complexion and answered, rather guardedly, 'Nay. I do not.'

I would have questioned her further—more out of curiosity than anything else—for I had yet to find someone who, even if they did not shun all gods as useless, believed in something other than the marble and wooden statues the Celts, Greeks, and Romans worshiped. However, Rufus and Aurelia were coming down the corridor, their laughter echoing in the peaceful stillness, so I did not ask Julia such a personal question. I noted that the pair had their hands intertwined, and I fought the urge to smile in amusement. Who would have thought it would happen so fast?

'Come, Marcella, we must be going,' Aurelia stated, letting go of Rufus. 'I have things waiting for me to attend to at home. Augustus will be home tonight, and I do not wish to miss him by being late.'

I rose to my feet, wishing I could have visited longer, and followed Aurelia to the door. Julia led us out with a smile, but I noticed a strange fear in her eyes—a fear that haunted my footsteps all the way back to the Aurelian villa on the Esquiline Hill, a fear that caused a single question to form in my mind.

Why? Did she believe in foreign gods? That was no excuse for fear. The Romans showed tolerance to all religions—

I halted in the street, causing Aurelia to give me a peculiar look.

One word sounded in my mind—a word I had heard often in the kitchen gossip, the name of a sect most hated and feared by all Romans, even more so than that of the Jews. Members of this sect were hunted down and put to death in the most horrible of ways. They were the cause of endless talk in the kitchens. That word, oft heard but never heeded, seared itself into my brain now and refused to vanish.

Christiani.

CHAPTER XIII

AGRIPPINA, WHAT DOST thou know of the Christiani?' I inquired as soon as the business of serving the evening meal had died away and peace once more reigned in the kitchens.

She looked up from cleaning the last of the dishes and stared at me. 'Now, Marcella, why shouldst thou of all people ask me that?'

I shook my head. 'Curiosity, that is all.'

She wiped her head with a soapy hand, the suds sticking to her forehead. 'Well, that will take some time indeed to relate.'

'I can wait.' I stepped forward and offered to help her.

'I thank thee kindly. Now then, once we are finished, I will tell thee all I know of that strange, mystical cult.' She shook her head, though whether in disbelief at my claim of sudden curiosity or something else, I did not know.

When the culina was clean, she sat down, adjusting her position in her chair and leaning back. I pulled up a stool and seated myself before her. The oil lamps had been snuffed out, and only the glowing embers of the fire thrust back the shadows of gloomy night. Every now and then, one of the wooden logs snapped under the heat and a shower of sparks would shoot up. All this formed the background to what Agrippina said, and I stared into the heart of the fire as she spoke, trying to retain the knowledge she gave me and satisfy my interest. She began to speak into the empty, flickering darkness of the kitchen.

'I know little, save rumor. But even that is enough to satisfy the most curious. I know not what they call themselves—only the name Romans invented for them. They are a religious sect that believe their leader, Christus, rose from the dead.'

I raised my eyebrows at the absurdity.

'Aye, I am telling thee the truth. Some years ago, during the reign of Emperor Tiberius—this was a few years before my time—there was a Jewish leader who claimed to be the Son of God. The Jews, of course, believed it heresy and had him condemned to death. The Christiani claim that their leader, Jesus, rose from the grave three days later, fulfilling many ancient prophecies. Members of this sect spread their religion throughout the Empire until the emperors began to fear that the Christiani would undermine their authority.'

'But I thought Romans believed in tolerance of other people's beliefs?' I ventured.

'Aye.' Agrippina brushed something off of her tunic. 'But only if those people are tolerant to the gods of the Roman emperors. The Jews, as everyone knows, are not so. Neither are the Christiani. Furthermore, the Christiani teach that no one except their God should be worshiped—not even the emperor.'

'Is that why so many of them are tortured to death in the new Colosseum?'

Agrippina nodded. 'The Christiani dishonor Rome by refusing to worship their gods and demean authority by refusing to burn incense to the emperor. But that is not all. They say that everyone is equal, be they man or woman, bond or free. The Romans do not believe that women and slaves should be granted equal status with men.'

'In my own country, women are respected as much as men,' I broke in, then closed my mouth, realizing too late that I had spoken my thoughts aloud.

Agrippina stared at me, but did not remark on my outburst. 'I suppose the one thing that aggravates Rome most is a ritual the Christiani perform.'

'What is that?'

She shrugged. 'No one knows, for no one can be a partaker of it unless they are one of that sect. 'Tis a celebration of their leader, and they eat human flesh and drink human blood as part of it.'

I snorted in disbelief. 'Surely not! Even the Romans are not so barbaric.'

'I know only what I have been told.'

'But then'—I glanced back at the flames, testing each word on my tongue before speaking it aloud—'they are cannibals—lawbreakers.'

'Aye, that is why they are so hated. Lawbreakers, and yet they cling to their religion with a tenacity that makes one wonder...' She shook her head. 'Marcella, thou shouldst go to sleep.' Agrippina rose to her feet and groaned, complaining under her breath of aching joints, and hobbled off to sleep.

I minded how the fire flickered away into darkness, reflecting my dissipating thoughts; my soul felt only disbelief. If that was all true about the Christiani, then....

I shook my head. It could not be so. How could people as kind and generous and well-to-do as Julia Maxima and her household be partakers in such barbaric acts?

I stumbled in the half-light of dawn the next morning, hastily washing with the rest of the bondwomen and eating some of the pottage Agrippina had prepared before going to Aurelia's chambers.

As she ate and I gathered her things in preparation for the daily walk to the baths, I had the boldness to ask her if we would be visiting Julia again that day.

'I think not, Marcella,' Aurelia replied sleepily. 'I promised Rufus I would try to read some of Virgil. Besides, Augustus will be dining here tonight one last time. His cohort is being called up to attend to some rebellion in the north.'

My heart quickened. 'Dost thou know where the rebellion is?'

Aurelia laughed scoffingly. 'Of course not. He never tells me things like that. I only know that he is going away.'

The thought crossed my mind that Lucius must also be going, as he was part of Augustus' cohort. A rebellion in the north? Was it in my own country? It might not be in Britannia—rebellions sometimes took place in Germania or Gaul. But, oh, what if it was?

A deep pang of the homing-hunger came upon me, and my hands trembled as they picked up Aurelia's things for the baths. I was relieved that she did not question my strange behaviour, for I did not know how I could have answered if she had.

True to her word, Aurelia remained within the confines of the Aurelian villa that day, taking up the scroll of Virgil's *Aeneid* and going to the peristylium to read, as the weather was warm and the sun once again shining.

I was serving in the kitchens after cleaning both the atrium and the dining room, silently working amidst the bustle of slaves rushing to and fro. As usual, something had gone wrong, and it put Agrippina in a foul mood. I was certain the Aurelian family was unaware of the many times they had nearly been poisoned due to a confusion of orders or some foolish accident on the part of a slave. Because it was Augustus' last dinner for quite some time, Agrippina was determined to do something more elaborate. This complicated matters tremendously, and I heard more than one servant complaining under their breath about it.

Without warning, a slave entered and rattled off, 'Marcella, thou art wanted in the atrium,' then departed just as quickly without an explanation.

I glanced at Agrippina in bewilderment and she jerked her head in the direction of the door. 'Twas best not to keep the mistress waiting.

I made my way up out of the kitchens and through the dying light in the peristylium. Aurelia was no longer there. I could scarcely see anything in the dim light until a slave came and lit the lamps, leaving me in silence. For a few moments I waited, searching the room to see who it was that had sent for me. Then I heard a slight scuffling, and a form arose out of the shadows, making its way towards me.

The figure thrust back the hood which obscured his face, and I saw at once that it was Lucius. He was dressed in the uniform of a legionary, the brass on his armor catching the light of the torches while his eyes remained in the shadows, dark and piercing.

I gasped in surprise.

'Marcella.' His voice was deep and soft, as if he did not wish for anyone else to hear him speak. 'Marcella, I have but a few moments to speak with thee. As thou might already know, our cohort has been summoned to reinforce the legions already stationed in Britannia to quell a rebellion of the Picts in the north. I do not know when I shall return, if ever.'

'Britannia.' I could barely force the word out.

'Aye. Our homeland.' There was a melancholy edge to his voice, a tone of regret that saddened his words strangely.

I blinked, a rush of warmth shooting through my veins. I suddenly realized that this was the first time since my captivity that anyone had spoken to me referring to something as *ours*.

'Marcella, I have a request to make of thee.' His voice now carried an urgency, and a throbbing sensation began in my chest, a mixture of curiosity as to what he could want to know and dread of what it might be. 'I wish to know this, at least, before I go…wouldst thou tell me thy British name?'

The blood drained from my face. Would no one cease to ask me that question? The Romans had replaced my name with another, never caring that I had a name before. Out of revenge, I had hidden it from them. They had destroyed my past; I could keep them from destroying it further. But Lucius was of my own people. He had treated me with nothing but kindness from the moment we met. And something within me longed for his friendship, impossible as it seemed. Could I trust him in this? Was I willing to tell him something I had kept secret for so long?

Voices grew loud in another room and I knew Aurelia would be impatient for my coming.

'Marcella, please?'

I looked him full in the face and knew, in some strange way, that I could trust him with this. He meant nothing cruel by it; only kindness, as he always did.

'My name is Enid,' I whispered, my voice barely audible, letting out a breath that I did not know I had been holding. And as I told him, an invisible weight lifted off of my shoulders.

'*Diolch*, Enid. Farewell.' Without another word, he bowed his head to me and then left, disappearing into the growing darkness of night.

I watched him depart, and in a moment, I knew something had changed within me.

My name, insignificant as it was, was my dearest treasure; that and my memories were the only things left to me that had not been stolen by the Romans. I could only give it freely, and yet it would always cost me something. To reveal my name now after so long meant putting the past behind me, yet I found I could still hold onto it and savor those shining memories, however dark the present might be. I had always known that should I ever reveal my true name, I would be giving a piece of myself away.

Yet I did not know, in that brief, passing moment, that I had given away my heart.

PART III

Sometimes I feel the fire
Satisfy this crippling nostalgia
Sometimes my heart is a liar
With nowhere to run but to you
Inside a failing desire
To put aside and forget it all
This time my mind conspired
So freely
What does it mean

CHAPTER XIV

TIME CEASES NOT in its ever-winding way, and summer dwindled away into the cooler months of autumn. I found the change of weather a great relief, for I could never grow accustomed to the intense humidity of a city with over one million inhabitants stifling beneath the relentless Italian sun.

The days went by slowly and yet, looking back, seemed to pass in a moment. Aurelia and Rufus spent more and more time together, and Julia and I were waiting for the day when Rufus would approach Aurelius—unless, of course, Aurelius had already arranged a suitable match for his daughter. Aurelia was scarcely sixteen, but most young women of her class were married at that age or younger. The pair of them seemed to think the matter settled already, though I knew only too well that nothing in life is ever truly certain.

As for myself, under Julia's patient tutelage, I learned how to read and write in the Latin tongue. While Rufus and Aurelia laughed together and grew in their friendship, Julia taught me the almost magical connection between symbols and sounds, and a whole new world was opened up to me. At last, I found a way to satisfy the never-ending hunger to learn more, and I voraciously read everything I could get my hands on, devouring Julia's library in my eagerness. I even risked Aurelius' wrath by reading works from his library; for I had asked Agrippina if I might begin cleaning that room of the house when needed. She had given me a puzzled look but consented. I do not know if Aurelia noticed, but even if she had, she never made an effort to stop me. Slaves often learned how to read and write; some had even risen to become teachers and scholars.

And so for the first time since I had been taken captive, I was almost satisfied with my lot in life. I lost myself in the realm of legends and stories of the Romans and Greeks, mentally changing the characters to the heroes of my people's mythologies. I also read the philosophers, subjectively taking sides in the many works of Plato, Aristotle, and others. I found myself intrigued and yet disgusted by Herodotus' *Histories*, for while he spoke in great lengths of many ancient cultures, my own was not mentioned. And Julius Caesar, who had written of the peoples he conquered on his many campaigns, did not always present an accurate representation of the northern tribes, and I was sorely tempted to take up a stylus and write the truth over his words.

In all that I read, one passage stood out to me more than the rest—even more than Herodotus' *Histories* and Julius Caesar's *Gallic Wars*: namely the scene in Virgil's *Aeneid* when the tragic hero, Aeneas, came in his wanderings upon the River Lethe, which runs through the Underworld. There lost souls came and had their memories erased in order to return to the world above; yet having once passed through the waters of Lethe, they could never return again.

I was like those lost souls. In my captivity and slavehood following, I had been separated from the world I knew and loved, my memories locked away to prevent them from being destroyed. All such sacrifices cost something, and mine had cost me much. I knew full well that I could never return to the world I had lost, for even if I found a way back, it would not be the same world that I had left....

Thus, even in all of this, I was not truly content. The longing for home still remained, though less sharp; it throbbed dully like an old, festering wound. I envied Aurelia less, for I found in Julia a kind spirit who was very much like myself with her desire for knowledge. She was kind to me, and willing to hear and answer my questions as best as she could. Yet I longed for something more. What, I could not say. Telyn, perhaps—yet I thought of him less and less as time wore on. Perhaps it was because I saw the fondness between Aurelia and Rufus and longed for it myself, knowing it could never be.

As the weeks wore on, Julia and I talked freely of the faith of the Christiani. I wished to know more about this hated sect, and Julia was more than willing to answer my questions. In these days, under Emperor Domitian, persecutions had become severe, but Julia trusted me; I was not the sort to babble to the Romans. In spite of the danger, she eagerly explained to me the tenets of her faith and I could understand now why the Romans misinterpreted it all.

I still could not understand why their God insisted they worship only Himself—for that sounded quite a lot like jealousy, and in that sense, He seemed no different from any other gods. Why would anyone risk worshipping one god above another if the deities were all the same?

But I did understand the rest of what Julia explained to me. The Christiani believed that they were all brothers and sisters of their leader, Christus, and that made them all of equal value, whether they be slave or free, poor or rich.

As for their mystic ritual, the Christiani were not eating flesh and drinking blood after all, but eating bread and drinking wine in memory of their leader's violent death. I believed Julia wished me to become one of them, but my curiosity had not yet grown to the point where I desired to attend one of their secret meetings—let alone join them. Their beliefs were still strange to me and, until I was willing to risk my life, I would not become one of them.

'Oh, Marcella!'

I looked up hastily from where I had been sitting, musing, and rose to my feet in an instant. 'Aye, Aurelia, what is it?'

She did not answer until she reached my side, but I could tell something of great importance had happened, for her face was flushed with excitement. 'Oh, Marcella, thou wilt never guess, so I might as well tell thee.'

'Tell me what?' I crinkled my brow in confusion.

'My father has betrothed me to Rufus Quintus Septimius.'

'What?' For a moment I was confused, as I had never heard his name in full before.

'Marcella!' She threw her head back and laughed, her soft dark eyes sparkling in delight. 'I am to be married to Rufus, of course!'

'Oh.' Not the most intelligent of answers, I admit. But I knew not what else to say.

Of course I wished her every happiness in life, but what would become of me? Would I remain in her father's household or would Aurelia take me with her to continue serving as her personal slave? Or worse, would I be sold to someone else?

'Why, Marcella, what's wrong?' The look of exuberant joy faded away from her face and concern took its place.

'Nothing, Aurelia. I do sincerely wish thee every happiness and joy in thy future life. I was only wondering what would become of me.'

'Thou wilt come with me to the Septimius villa, of course! Mater gave thee to me many years ago to do with as I please.

Besides, I think thou wilt enjoy having more time on thy hands instead of being under Agrippina's rule all day long.'

I nodded. 'I have never borne ill will towards Agrippina, for she has only been kind to me, but 'twill be pleasant to have more freedom.'

''Tis settled, then.' She smiled again.

'When is the marriage to take place?'

'Oh, a month before Saturnalia. By then, all the harvests will be in and Rufus will have finished his studies with his tutor and become the pupil to one of the leading rhetoricians—I cannot remember his name.'

'That leaves only a month for preparations,' I noted. I walked with Aurelia to the shadow of the columns in the peristylium where the crisp autumn winds could barely touch us.

'There is not much to be done. Mater has been preparing for my betrothal to someone for months.'

'How is it that thou wilt be living in the same house as Julia?' I could scarce fathom Aurelia being mistress of Julia Maxima.

'Because Rufus is the master of the Septimius villa. His father and mother both died of an illness some years ago and as Lucius—though the elder cousin—is illegitimate and cannot inherit, Rufus gains everything.'

'I see.' My face had inexplicably flushed at the mention of Lucius' name, and I turned away lest Aurelia should notice.

'Well, I must be off.'

'Where to?' I glanced up at her.

'To tell my friends the news,' she laughed over her shoulder. 'I will be home before *cena*.'

I watched her depart, her dark hair flying behind her in the wind, and then shivered, though not from the cold. I returned to the library on the upper floor and withdrew from its hiding place a scroll from Herodotus before tiptoeing my way to Aurelia's chambers. I had yet to finish his *Histories* and was somewhere in the middle of the account of the three hundred Spartans at Thermopylae.

I know not why I found that tale more interesting than the rest—perhaps it was because it put me in mind of the stories I had heard as a child of Boudicca's rebellion, of small hosts standing firm in the face of an overwhelming enemy, marching to their deaths because defeat would be worse than death. In that story, I found the same courage in the face of desperation that I remembered in my own people; anything that reminded me of home was precious to me, but especially this.

Opening it to the part where I had broken off earlier that day, I began to read, sitting in the corner of Aurelia's bedroom.

'...*The Barbarians accordingly with Xerxes were advancing to the attack; and the Hellenes with Leonidas, feeling that they were going forth to death, now advanced out much further than at first into the broader part of the defile; for when the fence of the wall was being guarded, they on the former days fought retiring before the enemy into the narrow part of the pass; but now they engaged with them outside the narrows, and very many of the Barbarians fell: for behind them the leaders of the divisions with scourges in their hands were striking each man, ever urging them on to the front. Many of them then were driven into the sea and perished, and many more still were trodden down while yet alive by one another, and there was no reckoning of the number that perished: for knowing the death which was about to come upon them by reason of those who were going round the mountain, they displayed upon the Barbarians all the strength which they had, to its greatest extent, disregarding danger and acting as if possessed by a spirit of recklessness....*'

I looked up and sighed with frustration. In place of the Persians and Greeks, I saw in my mind's eye only my people battling the Romans—battling Lucius. Chills crept up my spine at the thought. I did not want the only friend I had in the world to come to harm, especially at the hands of people I knew such as my brothers and Telyn. True, it was the Picts to the far north and not the Iceni that were the cause of the rebellion, but they were still Britons.

Did Lucius think the same? Did he feel guilt, slaying those who were from the land of his mother? Or did he think of them as strangers—Picts, the Brigantes, and Dumnonii—and not our people, unified by ancestral blood and the land we all lived upon and loved?

I stopped in my thoughts. Why should I care? Why did it matter to me how Lucius felt? Since when did it matter, and why did it matter so much?

I laid aside Herodotus and walked out of the room into the peristylium. Looking up at the sky, I watched the grey clouds suspended above the city like a misty cloak that hid the sun.

I wondered how long it had been since Lucius had taken Telyn's place. I had not noticed it, for it had been a slow change. But now it mattered—mattered much, though I did not quite know why.

I yearned to see him again, to ask him of my homeland. Only he could understand the longing, for he shared it as well. We were both caught between two worlds. He could never fully belong to either the Roman or British peoples; I could never be accepted by Roman society, even should I be freed, and my own people would be hesitant to accept me back. Lucius understood the pain of rejection and knew the emptiness of abandonment, but most importantly, he cared. He had shown kindness to me, kindness that had been repeated by his grandmother. I supposed that was what made him different from everyone else: not only did he pity me, but he understood my pain in a way that no one else ever could.

A sudden, painful throbbing coursed through my veins, startling me. What did it mean? I could not tell if my longing meant that I cared deeply for him—in the way my mother had cared for my father, in the way I had thought I cared for Telyn. Yes, Lucius had been kind, but only out of pity. It was ridiculous to imagine it could ever be anything more.

I shook my head as if to banish the thoughts that flooded my mind. I was mad. Such happiness was only for people in stories or people like Aurelia and Rufus.

I was not the fortunate protagonist. My story did not have a happy ending—not that I could foresee. I was the tragic hero, flawed and cursed. I could dream, but I could never hope.

Maybe, in the end, I was meant to be alone.

CHAPTER XV

THE DAYS GREW shorter as Aurelia's wedding approached, and at night the temperature dropped, though it was never as cold in Rome as in Britannia. One needed only a blanket or two in order to sleep comfortably, and the days were still warm. The trees were almost completely bare by the time the marriage took place, but I think that mattered to no one except me, for I had always loved the change of seasons and missed the vibrancy that Britannia displayed.

The night before Aurelia's wedding, the air was cool and no breath of wind stirred among the dying plants in the peristylium. I was among the few women with my mistress in the darkened atrium as she took off her *bulla* and toga praetexta and presented them before Lares, one of the Roman household gods. After the offering, she robed herself in a tunic of one piece—to be worn the next day at the wedding ceremony—and retired for bed.

In the morning, as the golden sun began to peep its yellow face through the mist over the waking city, all the women of the household went to Aurelia's room. I watched in fascination as Honoria arranged her daughter's hair by dividing it with a spear head into six strands, a tradition handed down from long ago when women were forced at spear point to become wives of the ancient Romans.

Then she fastened about her daughter's waist a band called the knot of Hercules, not to be untied until that evening, and only by Aurelia's husband. The other women jested good-naturedly at this until Aurelia's cheeks flushed crimson, but I did not take part in the banter, feeling out of place and embarrassed myself.

At last, draping Aurelia in the *flammeum*, the flame-coloured bridal veil, the women proceeded to adorn the bride with jewelry, ribbons, and a crown of flowers. Honoria hummed in approval and then led her daughter to the door of the house, the rest of us following behind.

At the door stood Rufus, adorned in toga and chaplet, escorted by his few relatives and many friends. Of course, Lucius and Augustus were not there, but I think their presence was hardly missed by any save myself amidst all the revelry.

As was the custom, the priests sacrificed a sheep and examined its organs, reading omens for the coming marriage. Fortunately for Rufus and Aurelia, they were favorable, and the pair entered into the atrium where they clasped each other's right hands while the customary ten witnesses and the wedding party gathered around them. Honoria stood between them to join their hands and hear them say the traditional vows, carried across the centuries of Roman history:

'*Quando tu Gaius, ego Gaia*'—Where thou art Gaius, there I am Gaia.

'*Quando tu Gaia, ego Gaius*'—Where thou art Gaia, there I am Gaius.

Then Aurelia asked, as was also the custom, 'Dost thou will to be my *pater familias?*'

To which Rufus consented and returned, 'Dost thou will to be my *mater familias?*'

After these vows of constancy, the pair took seats to the left of the altar, resting on the skin of the sacrificed sheep, while the priest made an offering to Jupiter and a prayer to Juno, asking them both to bless the couple and bring them a thriving marriage with many children.

At the conclusion of this ceremony, the wedding assembly congratulated Rufus and Aurelia with joyous cries of '*Feliciter!*'

Then came the wedding feast, of which we slaves were not permitted to partake. Nonetheless, we took our own repast in the kitchens with foodstuffs that Agrippina had carefully prepared with leavings from the banquet. Several of the male slaves became quite drunk and Agrippina hustled them out of her kitchen before they could cause a disturbance.

When all the feasting and celebrating was over, I was called to return to the wedding party as I was part of Aurelia's *dos*, or dowry, and would go with the couple to their own home. This procession, called *deductio*, was as much a part of the customary ceremonies as the oath-taking and sacrifice.

Aurelia was separated from Rufus with mock force by Honoria and taken to the front of the house. A youth clothed in white and holding a whitethorn torch in his hand led the way while two similarly dressed youths held onto Aurelia's hands. I walked behind her, carrying the distaff and spindle that represented Roman married life, and the acolyte who had served the priest carried the holy emblems and came after me. The rest of the wedding party followed, making all sorts of jests similar to the ones made by the women when dressing Aurelia much earlier, and everyone at odd moments cried out '*Talassio!*', invoking yet another god of marriage.

Rufus came to meet us, scattering chestnuts for the children as he went. The young ones, who watched the procession with good-natured curiosity, dashed in between members of the wedding party and scrambled to seize the nuts.

At the doorway to the Septimius villa, Aurelia wound the doorposts with symbolic wool and touched the door with oil and fat, offering a prayer for a life of plenty. After reciting *Ubi tu Gaius, ego Gaia*, she was lifted over the threshold and met in the atrium by Rufus, who presented her with fire and water, symbols of their new life together.

Aurelia took the whitethorn torch from the youth who had led the procession and lit the hearth. Afterwards, she threw it to someone in the crowd, who seized it and carried it off as a token of good fortune. Then Aurelia spoke another traditional prayer and was led by Honoria to the *lectus genialis*, the couch that stood in every atrium as a symbol of union.

The rest of us were sent away to bed, leaving Aurelia and Rufus alone. Honoria and Aurelius returned to their own villa. As for myself, I was quite exhausted by it all and, having been given a place to sleep in the upper story by Julia, closed my eyes and rested until morning.

No one woke me at the sun's rising and I slept in for the first time in years, being exhausted from the night before. When at last I opened my eyes, I rose hastily to my feet and dressed, going down the stairs to the peristylium. There I found Julia reading beneath the almond tree, the sun shining through the bare branches and creating dark, finger-like shadows on her pale lavender stola.

She looked up at my approach and smiled. 'Hast thou broken thy fast, Marcella?'

I shook my head, my senses still befuddled by sleep.

'Well then, come with me.' Julia stood up, laying aside the parchment and extending her hand to me.

She grasped my small, calloused hand in her larger, softer one. It was an unfamiliar sensation, but I did not shrink away from her. She took me to the kitchens and served me breakfast herself—a breakfast fit for those above my rank. When I began to protest, she smiled and shook her head, saying that she wished to spoil me for once. Without arguing further, I ate the bread and fruit eagerly, but I scorned the wine, never having grown accustomed to the peculiar taste.

Just as I was finishing, Aurelia entered the culina, clearly having returned from the baths, as her hair was damp. She spoke excitedly with Julia for several moments until she saw me. 'Oh, Marcella, didst thou rest well?'

I nodded, swallowing the last of the apricots. 'Didst thou?' I realized too late what I had said and looked down at my empty plate, my ears burning in embarrassment.

Aurelia laughed. 'Well enough.' She turned back to Julia and continued speaking with her, asking questions about whether she should leave the managing of the slaves to Julia until she had grown accustomed to her new life here or not.

When she finished, Aurelia looked at me and said, 'Marcella, wilt thou please unpack my things and put them in their proper place once thou hast finished eating?'

I rose and disposed of my empty plate. 'Where is thy room?'

'Oh, second door to the right of the atrium. My things are already in there, just not unpacked.'

I nodded once more and left the kitchens, pausing in the peristylium to drink in the warm November sunshine before continuing on my way. I craved sunshine and misty days in equal measure.

I found Aurelia's new bedroom dark after the light in the peristylium, but lighting the oil lamps in her chambers disposed of that problem. It was much grander than her room at the Aurelian villa. Beautiful frescoes adorned almost all the walls with pleasant countryside scenes from midsummer, making the place seem much larger and brighter than it really was.

Some might have found the chore she gave me tedious, but I did not think it so. In comparison with many things I had been assigned to under Agrippina, this was a light task and one that I enjoyed. And once I was finished, I could betake myself to the library or find company in Julia's presence.

An hour or so later, having completed my duty, I exited the premises and went out into the atrium where the sunlight dazzled blindingly on the rippling waters of the pool below the opening in the roof. The air was cool and crisp, and I inhaled it deeply, seeing in my mind's eye the golden colours of the leaves on the trees at my home far away in Britannia, and my breath caught in my throat.

I rarely thought of home, not only because it hurt too much, but because it was easier to live life and forget about what had been and what would never be. Yet in the odd moment or two when I did remember, the dull façade of contentment with my lot fell to pieces and I was once again vulnerable and lost in a world not my own.

Squeezing my eyes shut a moment as if to banish the thoughts that stripped away my mask of nonchalance, I continued through the corridor to the peristylium and paused.

Julia stood amidst the dying foliage in the garden, a sheet of crisp parchment forgotten in her hands. She was staring at something else, her face ghastly white and her eyes wide. The steward was by her side, and I supposed it was he who had delivered the letter—or whatever it was—to her.

I stepped closer, taking care not to make noise, but she heard me nonetheless and beckoned me to come to her, sending the steward away.

'What is it, Julia?'

Her smile trembled at the corners, and her eyes welled up with tears that she forced back. When she spoke at last, her voice was oddly stifled. 'I have just received a letter from the *milites medici* of Lucius and Augustus' cohort.'

'And what does it say?' I prompted. I felt as though the world was crashing in around me, darkness enshrouding the sunlight. Had something happened to Lucius? And if so, what? Was he all right? It was so long since he had called me by my true name, bidding me farewell in the Aurelian atrium....

Julia swallowed and looked down again at the letter in her hands, though I supposed she had read the whole thing enough times to memorize it all. 'There was indeed a rebellion on the northern frontier. Lucius' cohort was one of many sent to put it down...' She inhaled sharply before saying more. 'Augustus is well. But Lucius—' Her voice cracked and she tightened her lips. Her breath shook and the letter trembled in her hands.

My heart stopped beating for a moment and I willed her to continue, if only to know the worst.

'Lucius was severely injured in the conflict.'

'Is he still alive?' My breath caught in my throat and I clenched my hands at my sides, hoping the worst had not happened. The blood pounded so loudly in my ears that I could hardly hear Julia's reply.

Her gaze flickered up to meet mine. 'At the time this letter was written, he was.' She sighed, her voice tremulous and sad. She folded up the letter in her hands with great care, as if wrapping up her grandson so that he would be safe and well.

'What wilt thou do?' I could hardly keep the anxiety out of my voice. And there was a strange pain within my chest, very much like when I had awakened in the belly of the ship that had carried me away from my homeland.

'The milites medici wrote to inform me that if he recovers, they are sending him home once he is well enough to travel. There is no mention of the nature of the injuries—only that he will be of no further use to the army.'

If he recovers….

Surely that meant he was in danger of losing his life. It did not comfort me in the least. 'But what wilt thou do meanwhile? Do they even dare to risk sending a ship this time of year?'

'They have before. 'Tis a risky undertaking, but it has been done.'

'And thee?' I noted how she had skillfully avoided my question time and time again.

She smiled, a sad smile, but a strangely hopeful one all the same. 'I will pray to my God for Lucius' healing and protection.'

'And what if thy prayers be not granted?' I could not keep the doubt out of my voice. I did not yet share her beliefs or her meek assurance.

Her voice caught. 'Then such is His will. His grace is sufficient to heal the pain of such a loss.' Then she turned and left me.

I stood lingering there in the sunlight, my mind in turmoil. I did not know if I truly loved Lucius. Certainly I cared about him, for he was one of my own kind and he had shown me compassion; and his features were not unhandsome. But this longing for his safety—was it love or was it mere caring, as one friend cares for another?

In the midst of all my uncertainty, one thing was clear: I dearly wanted Lucius back home safely.

This realization showed me that I lacked something Julia had—the peace and comfort she seemed to find in her God. I had never minded having nothing to worship in all my years of slavehood until this moment.

Julia claimed that He was a good God, yet I was still afraid of trusting in Him. How could He let something terrible happen to Lucius, who also believed in Him? I did not understand Julia's peace and comfort, but I wished to have it now more than ever.

How could I bear to lose all that I loved yet again?

CHAPTER XVI

LIFE IS BLEAK for the hopeless, and I had no source of hope.

Aurelia seemed unaffected by the news once she knew that her brother was safe. Rufus was, I think, distraught at first, but the newfound joys of marriage distracted him from fear for his cousin's welfare. Julia spent hours praying to her God and otherwise retained an expression of peaceful resignation which I could not comprehend.

As for myself, I wandered dejectedly from chore to chore, constantly hoping that Lucius would be all right, as if wishing for it hard enough would make it happen. I yearned for someone to confide in, but it felt wrong to burden Julia with more grief. I longed to free the storm of emotions bottled inside me, but I could not. I could only endure the days that followed with a feeling of ominous dread in the air and the weight of the world on my shoulders, a weight that I could not shake off no matter how hard I tried.

Therefore, while the rest of the household prepared in great excitement for Saturnalia, I merely watched each passing day with fearful anxiety, waiting for news that never came. I caught a cold from sleeping with the window open one night, having forgotten to close it. I slept in my own room now, a luxury that Julia had given me, and while I enjoyed the quiet at night, I sometimes forgot to close the window or door, being accustomed to someone else always doing it. Julia advised me to rest so I would have the strength to celebrate with the other slaves during the festival—for the servants were treated as equals by their masters for this occasion once a year—but I refused, if only to prove to Julia's cook, Tullia, that I was not a sluggard.

Tullia was a brisk woman—much like Honoria—and she did not allow for any nonsense from any of us. I often missed Agrippina, for while she would not let us get away with shoddy work, she was also kind and sympathetic if any of us were ill instead of assuming it was an excuse to avoid work. I realized now how much I had taken her for granted, and I missed being questioned daily about my well-being.

'Marcella! Art thou coming?' Tullia's voice startled me back to reality and I tried in vain to ignore the pounding in my head.

'Aye,' I replied in a hoarse voice, rubbing my temples. I did not feel well, but I did not wish to be scoffed at for not celebrating the feast of Saturn with the others. It was already difficult for me to gain their acceptance, being a newcomer, and I did not wish to make things harder for myself. Those who shared Julia's faith went with the others only to avoid possible persecution, and I did not wish to remain behind and face ridicule—especially as I did not share the Christiani faith.

It was a rather rowdy group that left the house, but when we mingled with the others that thronged in the streets, we were hard pressed on every side and had little choice but to move with the crowd in the direction of the Forum. Once gathered around the Temple of Saturn, the roar of the people dimmed to a buzzing hum of voices as all heads looked up to where the priest prepared the sacrifice marking the beginning of Saturnalia.

I did not hear what the priest said, for I was too far away and my ears rang at odd moments. But it mattered little; most of those gathered were hardly paying attention to his words.

Then the sacrifice was made and the respectful quiet of the more devout Romans was shattered as the celebration began with a public banquet. Masters and slaves sat together, the masters serving their slaves. Food and wine were in abundance, and it did not take long before the merrymaking went wild. Gambling in the streets was permitted during the festival, and soon the dice—as well as the wine—flowed freely.

Julia, I noticed, did not laugh as easily as the rest, and I often caught her looking at nothing in particular, her eyes dark and sad. I wondered if she was thinking of Lucius, or whether the raucousness made her feel uncomfortable. As little as I knew of her faith, I did not think she would enjoy a pagan festival—

especially one that often turned into sheer madness before the week was over.

After an hour, when the majority of the feasting was over, Julia rose to leave, and I sought permission from Aurelia to join her as my headache was growing worse and I had difficulty breathing without coughing. She consented, and Julia and I made our way back home. It was slow going, forcing our way through throngs of dancing people who filled the streets, but once we ascended the Caelian Hill, the streets beneath cold, colourless skies were almost empty, the noise distant.

Once safe within the walls of the Septimius villa, I begged leave to lay myself down, and Julia placed a cool wrist against my forehead, putting me to bed herself. I sweated my way through a fever and distorted dreams and did not leave my room. Julia was kind enough to tend to me during the six days of the celebration, but I think she was glad of an excuse to skip the raucous merrymaking as much as I was.

During my days of recovery, I felt as weak and helpless as a young child and my patience quickly wore thin. It did not help that every passing day increased my worried anxiety for Lucius' well-being. When would they send him home, if ever?

More and more I found myself craving Julia's company. I yearned for the peace that she had. Surely, no other god I had seen or heard of provided its worshipers that kind of assurance and comfort, and I was almost willing to do whatever it took to gain it. Almost—I was not yet certain enough of Him to believe as completely as Julia did.

Often during those days of recovery, Julia would take me into the sunlight of the peristylium, carefully bundled up against the mild cold, and there read to me bits and pieces of what she said were the words of her God, copied from other manuscripts for her benefit. They were not much, but I supposed they were better than nothing. There was also a copy of a letter written by a man who had died for the same faith only a few years before I was brought to Rome—a letter he had written to the Romans. Julia read all these faithfully to me time and time again, patiently answering the many questions I threw at her.

Slowly, things began to become clearer. Due to my stubbornness and the way I clung to my stoic outlook on life, I found it hard to abandon my pride and simply accept what Julia told me as truth. But then again, perhaps it was also that I was afraid of trusting something—or someone—that might in the end let me down, just like everything else. It was a great risk; and the question, in the end, is whether such a risk is worth it.

As the days deepened into winter with no news of Lucius, I became desperate enough to read Julia's precious manuscripts on my own. I pored over them time and time again until I knew the words by heart, but still they seemed to me mere words and nothing more; I began to despair of them.

I became frantic as each night dwindled into an early darkness and still no word of Lucius was to be had. In my nightmarish dreams, the words of the Apostle Paul repeated themselves with haunting clarity until there was no solace to be found even in sleep.

'For the wrath of God is revealed from heaven against all ungodliness and unrighteousness of men, who hold the truth in unrighteousness; Because that which may be known of God is manifest in them; for God hath shewed it unto them. For the invisible things of him from the creation of the world are clearly seen, being understood by the things that are made, even his eternal power and Godhead; so that they are without excuse:

'Because that, when they knew God, they glorified him not as God, neither were thankful; but became vain in their imaginations, and their foolish heart was darkened. Professing themselves to be wise, they became fools. And changed the glory of the incorruptible God into an image made like to corruptible man, and to birds, and four-footed beasts, and creeping things....

'Who changed the truth of God into a lie, and worshiped and served the creature more than the Creator, who is blessed for ever. Amen....'

For me, it seemed, there was no peace, even if Julia and many of her servants found comfort in the words of the Apostle Paul. I found them cold and heartless. I was guilty of ungratefulness and failing to worship Julia's God, and if He truly did exist, I was destined for utter misery; that knowledge doggedly shadowed me even in the sober hours of the day.

Between the guilt and my fears for Lucius, my health began to crumble. Aurelia started to show concern, but I always avoided her questions—hers and Julia's. I was afraid of breaking, of appearing weak in their eyes.

Yet even I wondered how much longer I could bear the strain.

It was in the frosty days of late *Februaris* when it all came to its climax.

During the late afternoon one day, I had just returned from placing clean laundry in Aurelia's chambers when there came a deafening knocking on the double doors of the villa. At least, it sounded deafening to me—but by that point, my nerves were so worn that every noise not whisper-quiet made me skittish.

As the atrium was empty and no one else came to answer the knocking, I went to the door and opened it, peering out into the silver-grey twilight, my breath escaping in white, ragged gasps.

A man stood there, perhaps in his mid-forties, dressed in full army apparel and accompanied by a cluster of similarly-clad men. One of them leaned awkwardly to one side, staring at the murky city skyline with his back towards me.

My heart thudded to a stop and I glanced back at the man who seemed to be their leader.

'Is this the household of Rufus Maximus Septimius?'

I nodded, not trusting my voice to speak.

The leader said something over his shoulder, the words lost in the bitter wind. Then the man with his back to the door turned and limped towards me, leaning on a crutch. His face was hidden beneath a hood and his breathing was labored from the effort of dragging himself along. The other men walked away from the villa, leaving the cripple alone on the doorstep.

'May I come in, Enid?'

The blood drained from my face. I knew that voice. When I somehow found the courage to speak, my words were no louder than a whisper. 'Lucius?'

'Aye, Enid, 'tis I—or rather, what is left of me.'

It was strange hearing his voice again after so long; it almost seemed to me a dream. The world began to spin around me, growing farther and farther away. My knees buckled and I sank down, grasping the doorframe as if to hold onto reality before it, too, faded away into nothing. Black waters of oblivion came in at all sides, threatening to engulf me. From a distance, I heard something clatter to the floor, followed by raised voices, and I felt myself falling.

Then someone caught me in their arms and I knew no more.

CHAPTER XVII

WHEN I OPENED my eyes, I was in my room, lying down on my bed with the bedsheets pulled up to my neck. Sweat drenched my body and I struggled to free my arms to cool myself, my mind and body both sluggish.

'Shh, settle down. There is no rush,' I heard someone say, but I only saw a feverish blur of colours.

'Who's there?' My voice was hoarse, and soft like a dying breeze.

'Julia.' A new voice now, coming from somewhere farther off.

'And Lucius,' came the one that had spoken first.

I tried to say something else, but it sounded in my ears as only an incomprehensible moan.

'Go back to sleep, Enid,' Lucius said, his voice as gentle as it always was when he spoke to me, and then my world faded away once more.

One morning, I knew not how long after, I opened my eyes and saw with clarity for the first time since falling unconscious. My room was empty, but the door was open, and I could see out into the brilliant blue sky of early *Martius* that shone in through the roofless peristylium. A cross-breeze blew in from the open window above my bed to the world beyond my bedroom door, carrying with it the cold and earthy dampness that was spring. I could almost taste new growth in the scent of it.

Carefully, I hoisted myself up into a sitting position and leaned against the wall above my bed, feeling strangely at peace. Happy voices floated up from the peristylium below, borne upon the young spring wind. Birds twittered in the bare branches of the almond tree; the twigs were swollen with new buds, soon to break out of their dark prisons. And the sun shed its healing, golden rays upon a new world dawning out of winter's confinement.

'Marcella!' Julia's form shadowed the door and she came towards me with a pleasant smile on her face. Laying her wrist on my forehead, she said, ''Tis a great comfort to see that thou hast wakened at last. Indeed, many times we feared we had lost thee.'

'How long have I been in the fever?' My voice was raspy, but it was louder than my previous attempts to speak.

'Nigh on two weeks. Aurelia looked in on thee at times, and Lucius never left thy side.' She stepped back, gazing at me with that same sweet smile. 'But I think thou art on the mend now.'

'What happened?'

'*Enid!*'

Lucius stood in the doorway. He was leaning on his crutch, an overjoyed—almost relieved—smile on his face. He limped towards me, grimacing with pain when he put too much weight on his bad leg and forcing the look of pain away with great difficulty.

I watched him, still struggling to believe that he was really here and not lying dead upon British ground as I had feared for so long. He was here, sitting beside me, calling me by the name I had heard from no one in so long.

'Enid, thou art better?'

If Julia noticed that he did not call me Marcella, she said nothing; perhaps he had already told her, when I was sick. In any case, I did not mind it—though I would have disliked it coming from anyone else.

'Aye,' I replied. 'At least, I feel better than I did before.'

'Well, that is a good thing.' Julia handed me a cup of cold water. 'Drink this.'

I took it from her and drank it, choking down the bitter taste of herbs and handing back the empty cup. 'What happened?' I asked again.

Lucius and Julia glanced at each other before Lucius responded, 'When I told thee it was I at the door, thou seemed to undergo some sort of strange shock. Thou didst fall to the floor—'

'Lucius and I caught thee,' Julia interrupted, 'else thy head would have smashed against the pavement.'

Lucius shifted his position, looking at the floor as if to concentrate on what he said. 'We placed thee in thy room and sent for the physician. He said thou wert under too much strain and that there was little hope of thee ever regaining consciousness. I do not believe thou wert properly awake again until now,' he concluded, glancing up at me with concern—and something else I could not lay my finger on.

'I remember waking sometimes, but it was all so far away and distant,' I replied after a moment.

Julia brushed aside the hair that hung over my eyes. 'Well, it seems thou art on the mend, but I think thou shouldst sleep a bit more. Thou canst talk later after thou hast rested. I do not wish to have to endure more scares from thee due to exhaustion.'

I nodded meekly and slipped back under the covers. I was indeed very tired, though I had been sleeping only a few minutes ago.

Lucius rose to his feet and limped out of the room, glancing at me over his shoulder, the corners of his mouth upturned in an encouraging smile. The sight of him filled me with a warmth words could not describe; I was glad he had returned safely back home.

Julia pulled the covers up to my neck and tucked them snugly around me. Whatever she said was lost as I closed my eyes in a refreshing, dreamless sleep.

It was indeed much more than a few hours before Julia at last permitted me to rise from my bed. I was glad to be out of my room and washed and dressed in clean clothes. Julia pampered me almost as if I was her own child. She had supplied Aurelia with a substitute servant so that I was not missed during my illness, but Aurelia often came to see how I fared, which was kind of her.

Having given me some sort of broth, Julia took me out into the peristylium and read to me from Homer's *Odyssey* while I drank in the freshness of the spring. It was not as glorious as spring in Britannia, but it was a beautiful and welcome change nonetheless. Julia's gentle voice, reading the rolling, poetic lines of my favorite work, was soothing, and I closed my eyes, feeling the sun's warmth enliven me.

A shadow fell across me and I opened my eyes to see Lucius blocking the sunlight. Julia paused in her reading, and for a moment we heard the songs of the birds distinctly in the tranquility.

'Dost thou mind?' He gestured to the empty space on the marble bench beside me.

'Nay.'

With difficulty, he lowered himself down, holding onto his crutch as a beam of support until he was seated.

Julia looked at the pair of us for a moment and then excused herself, rolling up her scroll and leaving us alone in the spring sunshine.

'What happened—in Britannia?' I asked after a period of silence.

'Many things, Enid.' His voice was soft, his eyes far away.

I waited for him to continue, studying how the sunlight shone on his dark hair, the ebony nearly blue.

'For one, I saw thy family.' A note of wry amusement entered his tone.

'Thou…what?' The air was knocked out of my lungs by his words.

'Aye. While we were stationed in Venta Icenorum, I walked up into the hill country and came to thy village. It was not the first village that I visited in hope of finding thy tribe. It took some time, but I found thy family and spoke with them, telling them that thou art still alive. As might be expected, they did not believe me—or trust me—at first. Some part of me still doubts whether they believed me in the end.'

'How are they?' I could not keep my voice from trembling. It was odd to think of my family still existing in that world that was no longer mine. It had been so long since I thought of them; I felt as if I had always been a slave and the memories of my past were only a dream.

A smile played on Lucius' lips. 'They are well, though missing thee still, I think. Thy two eldest brothers are married and two of thy sisters also, they tell me. Thy youngest brother is yet learning the harping skills from Caradoc.'

Throbbing warmth shot painfully through my veins at the news, bringing back all the longing for home that I had thought buried forever.

'And Telyn?' The words escaped from my lips before I realized it.

'Wedded to thine eldest sister. He asked after thee, but how didst—'

I shook my head. 'I fancied myself in love with him once. We would have been wed had I not been captured by the Roman traders.' *Telyn. Could it possibly be true?*

What surprised me most was how peacefully I received the news. I felt none of the heartache I expected—only acceptance and a strange comfort knowing that Telyn was happy and had moved on, even as I had, in my own way.

'Then thou must hate me for bringing this news to thee.' His voice was sympathetic, but there was a hard edge to it, like the scraping of blade against blade.

'Nay, I do not hate thee. I do not care for him in that way now. I learned long ago that I had to let go in order to survive in Rome. One cannot always be held down by thoughts of what might have been.'

'Still, 'tis a tragic thing.' That edge was still there.

I shrugged. 'I have learned to live with such losses.' I inhaled sharply, my breath shuddering, for it still made it no easier to endure such pain when it threatened to destroy my world again. 'What else happened in Britannia?'

'This.' He lifted up his injured leg, and I saw for the first time that it was twisted and malformed, the skin horridly discoloured. 'On our march to the North, we encountered a large company of the Painted People. I slipped and fell beneath an oncoming chariot. Thou canst imagine the rest.' He laughed bitterly. 'I am useless now.'

'I am sorry,' I said at last. I knew not what else to say, and it seemed wrong to say nothing at all.

'I shall learn to live with it, I suppose.'

An awkward silence fell between us again.

'Enid, may I ask thee something?' Lucius questioned softly.

'Aye.'

'What distress was it that caused thee to become ill?' He spoke hesitantly, testing each word on his tongue before speaking them. 'Thou dost not need to tell me if thou dost not wish it,' he added hastily.

'Nay, I do not dread it.' I paused before continuing on. ''Tis only that...a great many things were the cause of it, and thou might think some of them foolish.'

'Then thou art wrong,' Lucius reprimanded gently, his voice deeper. His voice always seemed to jump octaves lower when he spoke softly. 'I would never think thee silly. Whatever it was, it distressed thee greatly and therefore is nothing to laugh at.'

I nodded my thanks and waited, trying myself to untangle the mess of worrisome thoughts that flooded to mind. 'Well, there was the longing for home and the excitement of the new changes that came with Aurelia's wedding. And then Julia—nay, it began before that. She received news that thou wert injured, possibly to death…and I was afraid that thou wouldst never come home.' Despite my attempts to control my voice, it trembled against my will.

Lucius reached out with his hand and brushed my own, the touch of his fingers sending a wave of warmth washing over me. 'I am home now,' he whispered, and I felt his breath against the side of my face.

'Aye.' I took a deep breath before continuing, hoping he did not notice how my face flushed. 'I once asked Julia how she could be so hopeful. She attempted to explain her faith to me, even reading some of her scriptures to me, but it only made it worse. I was in a constant state of terror, and even in my sleep, my dreams were tormented with visions of God's wrath. I—I felt hopeless. I still do.' I exhaled, feeling a great weight lift off my shoulders at speaking my heart at last.

'Enid.'

The way he said my name always sent the strangest sensations through me, sensations I had only felt with Telyn—the thought unnerved me.

'Enid, thou didst only reach the threat of what will happen to those who continually reject God. There is hope for His redeemed.'

'And what if I am not one of those redeemed?'

'Do not say that; I refuse to believe it.'

'But what if it is true?' I looked him full in the face, the frustration rising within me as it did every time I asked myself this question.

Lucius sighed and seemed to stare at something I could not see. 'Thou wilt long to know Him if He is reaching out to thee… Oh, Enid, I will not give up on thee and neither will God. Thou needest only to surrender thyself to Him, everything that thou art, and then thou wilt find the peace that Julia and I possess.'

'A simple act, yet such a great sacrifice,' I mused.

'But it is worth it all.' He shifted his crutch under his arm and rose unsteadily to his feet. 'I must go, but I wish to speak to thee soon.' He bowed his head and left me alone in the spring sunshine to muse over what he had said.

Much had changed in those short minutes. I had news of my family, vague as it was—news of Telyn. It was strange how long I once hoped that somehow I would win back to home and we would be wed. Despair had killed that desire. Though I still hoped one day I could call myself my own, I had accepted this fate of mine; that was how I could accept the news of Telyn being married to my sister. But I think there was also another reason that that news did not hurt me in the slightest—even if it did leave me shocked.

Lucius.

He also had undergone much change. He had returned to the land of his birth and come back crippled. I noted how he did not say whether his people had welcomed him as one of their own or rejected him because of the Roman blood that flowed in his veins. The proud gold of the Redcrest blood interwoven with the pure silver of the ancient Celts—an almost sacred mingling, yet forbidden to coalesce with either of the peoples from which it had sprung. He too was caught between two worlds, belonging to neither. Perhaps that was why, from the first, I had felt more compassion for him than any other Roman.

Julia had told me that the chariot crushed the bone of his leg to splinters and it would never fully heal. Lucius was not one to complain, but I wondered how he managed to bear the pain—and the shame. He had joined the army to prove his worth to the Romans and yet lost what little worth he once had in their eyes.

'Marcella?' I looked up from my musings to see Julia walking towards me, an expression of motherly concern on her face. 'Wouldst thou like to lie down for a while? Thou art still very weak.'

'Aye, I would like that very much.' I rose, stiffly, and returned to my room, leaning on Julia for support.

She laid me down and left me, the window still open to allow the fresh spring breezes to enliven my room. I closed my eyes, feeling the slight tension in my muscles relax. Ever since I had allowed my fears to take control of me, I had lost what pride and strength remained to me. It would be a long time before I regained my former vitality, and meanwhile I would have to rely on the people of the nation I despised most for everything, as a baby would her mother.

Yet even as the world around me faded into a peaceful darkness, I realized that I no longer despised them.

In my heart of hearts, I had even begun to love them.

CHAPTER XVIII

MARCELLA!' AURELIA'S VOICE rang out through the atrium, and I looked up from Homer's *Odyssey* to see my mistress coming towards me.

I rose and laid aside the volume I had been reading. 'Aye, Aurelia, what is it?'

As she came towards me, the warm *Aprilis* sun dazzled off of her crimson stola, the embroidered gold sparkling in the light. 'Marcella, art thou well enough to accompany me to my father's house?'

I knitted my brow in confusion. 'Why, whatever for?'

'I wish to pay a visit to my mother and I thought thou mightest like to accompany me. Unless, of course, thou dost not,' she added hurriedly.

I was taken aback by her thoughtfulness. 'I would have to ask Julia if I am well enough to walk such a distance yet,' I murmured softly, unsure how to respond to being given a choice. I had not been my own mistress for so long that the privilege of making my own decision felt unnatural. I did not know how to properly respond. 'Though 'twould be nice to see Agrippina again,' I added, more to convince myself than her that I was willing to go.

'My thoughts exactly,' Aurelia returned. 'Do let me know soon, for I wish to go this very day. I have news for her that cannot wait.' She flashed an animated smile and left the atrium, her stola fluttering behind her like the wings of a scarlet butterfly.

'As thou wishest.' I bowed my head and went in search of Julia. On the way to the kitchens—where I suspected her to be at this hour of the morning—I nearly collided with Lucius, who was passing in front of the kitchen stairs.

'Aiee! Thou art in a hurry!' he exclaimed, leaning against the wall to regain his balance. His face was white with pain.

'I am so terribly sorry,' I apologized hastily, 'but Aurelia wishes me to accompany her on a visit and sent me to ask Julia's permission…I thought it best not to waste time in asking.' The last phrase was forced out, guilt rising at the twisted grimace on his face. How badly had I hurt him, I, who cared about him so deeply?

'Quite right.' Lucius stuck his crutch under his right shoulder, changing his support from the wall to the stick. He drew in his breath sharply at the movement, and my guilt grew even greater.

'I am sorry I did not see you,' I said awkwardly. I did not know what to say. My heart did, but I feared how he might

198

respond. The torture of loving and not knowing whether my love was returned was better than knowing it was rejected.

'Nay, 'tis no great matter.' His voice was dead even, a sharp contrast to the emotions warring in my own heart.

'Does it hurt much?'

Lucius glanced up at me, his eyes dark. 'There are times when I hardly notice it at all. And then there are times when I think life would be easier if I had died.'

'Do not say that—do not say life would be easier if thou wert dead!' The words flew out of my mouth before I could stop them, and a miserable blush spread across my face. What must he think of me?

'What makes thee say so?' There was a note of curious trepidation in his voice now, though there was more fear than anything else.

'Julia would miss thee...and so would I.' I had already exposed myself; a little honesty would not do much more damage than had already been done.

'Thou wouldst miss me?' His tone was incredulous, but I dared not meet his gaze. Not now. I was afraid of what I would see there.

When I did find the courage to speak, my words were heated. 'Of course I would! Besides Julia and Agrippina and Aurelia, thou art the only one to show kindness to me. And thou alone out of all of them canst understand my pain—the loneliness of being lost, belonging to neither the Roman world nor the British one. Thou alone canst speak my tongue. Thou alone cared about my Celtic heritage. Thou alone saw that I had worth when no one else did…I know that thou must think little enough of me, and perhaps thou believest that I think little of thee, but it is not so with myself.'

I tried to walk past him, but he reached for my arm with his free hand to keep me from leaving.

'Enid, wait.'

'Whatever for?' I turned, trying in vain to hide the hot tears threatening to spill down my face. I was ashamed of having revealed so much of my soul to him; I did not want him to see me cry now.

'Enid, listen to me. I know all those things which thou sayest, for they are true. In thee I have found a comfort no one else could give because thou understood what they could not. But thou art wrong about one thing. I do not think little of thee at all.' He sighed and his grip on my wrist slackened slightly. 'All those things—nay, all the kindness that I have shown to thee— it was not merely for my own pleasure. I did not wish to know of thy lineage and family, thy culture and heritage simply because I desired to know more about the people from whom I too was forcibly estranged. Aye, I wanted to know, but I did not do those things for myself alone. I did them for thee! I did them because I know what it is like never to belong, never to be understood, never to feel wanted, and I wished to be a friend to thee. No human being should ever feel such loneliness and sorrow, least of all thee.'

He released me, his arm dropping limply to his side. 'I will not hinder thee longer,' he said, the passion vanishing from his voice like fog in a sunrise. As he left, I noticed how his injured leg seemed to drag more than usual.

I wandered down to the kitchens, but my mind was in such turmoil that I merely stood there on the steps for many minutes, staring dumbly at the entrance to the rooms below.

'Why, Marcella, whatever is the matter?'

I jumped in surprise and looked up at Julia. 'Oh, Aurelia wishes me to go with her to visit her mother today. Dost thou think I am well enough to go?'

'Aye, but do not stay out too long.' She searched my face for a moment. 'Art thou certain that is all that troubles thee?'

'There is something else, but I do not wish to speak of it now.'

'Well then, I must not keep thee.' Julia smiled encouragingly and continued up the stairs.

I turned on my heel and followed her more slowly, my thoughts racing wildly. What *had* happened? What did Lucius' words mean? Perhaps I had been wrong all this time. He claimed he had been compassionate out of pity, but I did not think pity strong enough to evoke such a passionate outpouring of words. Yet if it was more than pity....

I felt my face grow hot.

Nay, it could not be.

It was strange to return to the place where I had spent the last four years of my life. I knew it so well, yet after being gone for a few months, it felt odd to be back again. Honoria took scarcely any notice of me—her interest was in seeing her daughter and not her daughter's personal slave—so I slipped down to the kitchens for a chat with Agrippina as soon as the opportunity presented itself.

Agrippina had not changed in the past three months, and she seemed glad to see me. 'Marcella! 'Tis a good thing to see thee again!' She set aside the bread she was kneading to rise and bade the other servants leave the culina.

'And 'tis good to see thee.' I smiled, realizing suddenly how rare it was that I did so; perhaps my illness had begun to strip away my emotionless mask. 'How hast thou been?'

'Good, as always. Not much has happened of interest, save that Althea and Rastus finally wed. Old Silvius has been much abed this winter because of his aching joints—there is talk that he might be released from service, as he cannot do much. Life is a good deal quieter now that thou and Aurelia are gone.' She wiped the back of her hand across her sweaty forehead and sat down on the chair by the glowing embers of the kitchen fire. It was quite warm in the kitchen, even without the roaring flames that usually burned on the hearth. 'And what of thee and thy new household? Do the other servants treat thee well?'

I hesitated, looking at the patch of watery sunlight that spilled in from the open doorway onto the rough stone floor. 'They treat me well enough. But I know little of the household gossip, as I have been ill these past several days.'

'Ill? Why, Marcella, with what?' Her voice, at that instant, reminded me so much of my mother.

'A fever,' I replied simply.

'A fever that lasted several days? 'Tis unusual.' Agrippina creased her brows worriedly.

'I…I was weakened beforehand so it lasted longer than it would have otherwise.'

'Marcella, what happened?'

I could hardly bear the pleading concern in her tone.

'Many things.' I paused for a moment. 'I received bad news, and worrying about it wore me down—then I had a shock one day and I lost consciousness, becoming ill.'

'Why didst thou not speak of thy fears to someone? Mistress Julia has been very kind to thee—why didst thou not confide in her?'

'I was afraid of burdening her. She was worried also. I did not wish to give her more weight to carry.'

Agrippina rose to her feet, her arms crossed. 'Then that is where thou art wrong, Marcella. Sharing thy concerns with someone is never a burden. It is only a burden upon thyself and other people when thou holdest it all in. Thou hast only thy stubborn pride to blame for thy sickness. Keeping thy fears to thyself does no one good, especially thyself. Please promise me to never do so again.' Her voice softened at the end and I nearly thought she would cry.

'I promise,' I said, wondering how difficult that promise might be to keep.

Agrippina seemed about to say something else when Aurelia called me. I straightened from leaning against the table. 'I must go.'

'Ah well, Marcella. Keep in mind what I said.' She smiled kindly, but there was a touch of sadness in her gaze that I did not fully understand. Perhaps it was pity, but I was not certain.

Returning up the stairs, I met Aurelia and we walked together in silence to the atrium.

Honoria embraced her daughter tightly. 'Do let me know if thou needest anything! Tell me any news that thou hast.'

'I will, Mater.' Aurelia laughed lightly. 'There is much time yet.'

'Even so, I wish to know.'

'*Valdete*, Mater.' Aurelia smiled.

'What was that about?' I ventured once we were beyond earshot of the Aurelian villa.

'Oh, I am with child,' she replied with as much concern as if speaking of how bright the sun was over our heads.

I stared at her, not knowing what to say. Of course, I should not be surprised—after all, it was the natural conclusion of marriage. Yet it was odd, if only because she was a few years younger than me, and I was not even betrothed. But then, I doubted I would ever have the chance to wed. Lucius' face came to mind and I squeezed my eyes shut in an attempt to push it away. I could not—I must not—think of it.

'I am very happy for thee,' I managed at last, trying to sound cheerful for her sake.

I truly wanted to be kind towards her, yet my heart burned with a desire to be loved the way Aurelia was loved by Rufus.

That night, I was awakened out of a deep slumber by a scream. Sitting upright, I strained my ears and heard only silence for a few moments. Then came a dreadful groaning, as of someone in deep distress.

Thrusting aside the bedsheets, I rose and slipped out of my room, pausing in the corridor to listen for the noises in an attempt to find their source. I heard another groan—coming from the room beside mine.

The one that belonged to Lucius.

Without hesitation, I opened the door, which was unlocked. The room was dimly lit by a single oil lamp on a small table by his bed—perhaps he had forgotten to snuff out the light before falling asleep. His crutch was leaning against the wall by the table, its shadow huge and misshapen in the darkness. As for Lucius, he was fast asleep and covered in sweat, his tunic and bedclothes clinging to him. Every few moments, those same groans and screams which had awakened me in the beginning escaped his lips.

Crossing the room in a few strides, I touched his arm and called his name, but he did not so much as stir. At a loss for what to do next, I took up a cup of water from the table beside his bed and flung the contents in his face in another attempt to awaken him.

Gasping, he jerked upright, rubbing his face. He stared, blinking at me and the cup in my hand. 'Enid?'

'I—I am sorry, Lucius, but I did not know how else to awaken thee.'

'I was screaming again, was I not?' His voice was dead and emotionless.

'Has it happened before?' I had never heard it, but then, I had been ill.

'Aye.' He placed his head in his hands and groaned softly, running his fingers through his tousled hair, dark strands sticking to his damp forehead. 'It has happened before.'

'What is the cause of it?' I sat down on his bed and shivered, feeling the chill from the mosaic floor seeping through my bare feet.

Lucius sighed. 'Nightmares.' He straightened and leaned back against the headboard. 'Memories of what happened in Britannia. It comes back after dark, remembrances of the battle—and what followed after.' He did not meet my eyes, but gazed dully at the sheets, his hands fiddling with them.

I was silent. If he wished to speak of it, he would tell me of his own free accord. I would not force it from him.

'Enid, hast thou ever heard the tales of warriors in battle and their glorified songs of honourable deeds?'

I shrugged. 'Have not we all?'

He laughed bitterly. 'They are wrong, so…wrong.' The last word was barely audible. 'In the heat of battle, thou dost not think about anything except the moves of combat, fighting to survive. Battle-frenzy, some call it, for it is a twisted madness. Killing, seeing thy comrade's face torn open and bleeding everywhere, the awful carnage left by chariots riding over bodies and crushing them further. Arrows and spears split the air, whistling and shrieking like Gwyn ap Nudd and his Wild Hunt our harpers sometimes sing of.' He shuddered. 'But the worst is after the battle…the screams of the dying, the calls for help that are never answered, the groans of those who have no way to end the pain.' His voice caught in his throat. 'Waiting to be carried off the field after I was injured was a living hell. Drifting in and out of consciousness only to hear those sounds…death seemed welcome in those hours, and I longed for it to take me.' He shook his head. 'In my dreams, it often comes back and I have no means of escape.'

'What can I do?' My voice was small and insignificant.

He looked up at me, his face shadowed in the flamelight, and smiled faintly. 'Wake me up when it happens again. Speak to me, make me think of something else. 'Tis the only thing that helps.'

'I shall try,' I replied simply.

The faint smile still rested on his lips. 'I thank ye, Enid. But come, the night waxes late and thou needest thy sleep. Thou art still recovering.'

I rose to my feet as he slipped again under the bedsheets, but I hesitated in the doorway, my hand on the plastered wall. 'Lucius?'

'Aye, what is it?'

It was a moment before I answered, for I did not want to hurt him. 'Dost thou think thou wilt ever walk again—without thy crutch?' I tried to read his gaze in the dim, flickering light.

'I do not know,' he said after a while. 'They did not even expect me to live…they gave me no hope of walking normally again. Sometimes I think that I might, one day, but then the pain comes again and I doubt it.… Why dost thou ask?'

I shrugged. 'I do not know, only that thou seemest oft to be in great pain.'

''Tis not for thee to concern thyself with. It is my struggle and mine alone. I appreciate thy concern, Enid, but I doubt it will ever be like it was before. We can never go back.'

A moment of silence fell between us, his words echoing in my mind. *We can never go back.* How bitterly true it was. 'Good night, Lucius,' I said at last, turning to go.

'Good night, Enid,' I heard him say before the door closed and I was left in the chilly darkness of the empty corridor.

I did not return to my room immediately, standing still in the hallway overlooking the starlit peristylium. *It is my struggle and mine alone*. How often had I said those words myself, speaking of my own pain and suffering? I was almost angry with Lucius for holding himself aloof, wrapping himself in his own brokenness, instead of reaching out and letting himself be loved and cared for by those who wished for his happiness. Yet I could not blame him, for I was guilty of the same. We were both broken and wounded by the hardships of life; but perhaps, together, that brokenness could be healed and made new.

CHAPTER XIX

MARCELLA? IS SOMETHING wrong?' Julia's voice broke into my musings and I looked up to see her coming towards me.

As I continued to regain my health, I had slowly resumed my duties as Aurelia's maidservant and found that the yoke of slavery being placed upon my shoulders again after a period of freedom was almost a grievance. Lucius kept himself at a distance from me—a wall seemed to have come between us since that night he had awakened out of nightmares and spoken with me. The days had grown dull, and even the stories I had once loved became stale, their words meaningless.

Julia sat down beside me on the marble bench warmed by the sun. A slight, cool breeze played in the budding branches of the almond tree, scattering the pale pink blossoms.

'Nay, I do not think so,' I responded, the parchment in my hands slipping out of my fingers. I caught it and rolled it up carefully, placing it beside me lest it fall to the ground again.

''Tis only that thou seemest very listless these days. Is there nothing that can make thee smile again?'

As if I ever smiled freely before, I thought, but did not voice it aloud. Jealousy and bitterness warred in my heart and I did not want it spilling out in unnecessary wrath. 'I do not know,' I said at last in a small voice. 'I am discontented, but I do not know why.'

I was lying. I knew full well that I was jealous of Aurelia and Rufus and their happiness, believing I had little hope of ever experiencing that kind of joy.

'Is it because of Aurelia?'

I stiffened, my face flushing. 'What makes thee say that?' I dared to glance up and saw her looking at me, pity in her eyes.

Then she smiled. 'Thou art close in age to her, and I know that thou art a very passionate person. Thou hast a fierce love, like all thy kind, but perhaps thou hast no one to bestow thy love upon—or perhaps thou dost, but thou dost not find thy love returned?'

The blood rushed to my face again and I fidgeted with the hem of my slave's tunic. Could she have guessed how I felt about Lucius?

As if she could indeed read my thoughts, she continued, 'I have seen the way thou gazest at Lucius, nor did I think thy concern over his survival was merely because he was a fellow Briton.'

I opened my mouth to speak, but found I could not. Yet even if I could speak, what would I say? To deny it would make me even more of a liar and to tell the truth would be to open myself up and oh! how I was afraid of that!

Julia took my hand in hers and caressed my fingers gently with her own. 'Thou dost not need to be ashamed, Marcella. I am glad that thou carest for him in such a way; few people have ever accepted him. As for where his heart lies, that I do not know. Methinks he is afraid to let himself love anyone after what happened in Britannia. But do not give up hope. Thou hast much love to give. Do not lock it away.'

She rose to her feet. 'Wouldst thou like to come to one of the Christiani's meetings?'

'I do not know if Aurelia would wish me to be out after dark. I would have to ask her permission. Yet I thank thee all the same.' I attempted to smile, but it felt forced. My thoughts were in turmoil.

'Why does Lucius call thee Enid?' she asked, as if it were an afterthought.

'Because it is my British name. He asked me what it was before he went away to Britannia.' How long ago that seemed now.

Julia smiled sweetly. 'Enid—does it not mean purity?'

A smile, a genuine one this time, formed on my own lips. 'Aye, it does. I loved my name. Marcella means nothing to me.'

There was a twinkle in Julia's eye, but I noticed that she was looking beyond me and I turned to see Lucius approaching. 'Lucius, what does Marcella mean?' she asked of him as he drew nearer.

'It means strong warrior.'

I was acutely conscious of him standing next to me and an uncontrollable blush spread across my face. Why could I never keep a nonchalant manner when in his presence?

'See,' Julia pointed out. ''Tis not a name to be ashamed of, be it Roman or no.'

'Avia,' Lucius began to speak, but I never heard the rest. My discomfort overcame me and I rose to my feet, slipping away before either of them could call me back. Aurelia would be wanting me, and besides, I did not belong in their private conversations.

'Marcella?'

I halted on the steps to my room, my hand resting against the cold, damp wall. 'Aye, Julia?'

'Dost thou wish to go with me tonight to one of our meetings?'

'Avia, thou must not go—I forbid it.'

I turned around to see Lucius shadowed by the torchlight, worry etched on his face. He laid his free hand on his grandmother's shoulder as if to prevent her from walking out to the atrium.

'Lucius, why?'

'Thou knowest as well as I that Emperor Domitian doth not look kindly on those of our faith. It is said that soon his persecutions will rival even those of Nero's day.'

'I know all this, *mea nepos*. I am well aware of the costs of following Christus. But that will not stop me.'

'Avia, listen to me! If thou art caught, they will show no mercy, regardless of thy station in life. Hast thou heard tell of the barbaric manner in which we Christiani are put to death?'

'Lucius!' I had rarely seen Julia so angered. 'I know all these things. Yet Christus Himself said that those who followed Him would be hated by the world because the world hated Him. 'Twould be an honour to die in His name.'

'Aye, but without thought to thy family, to those that are dependent on thee?'

Their voices softened and I had to strain my ears to hear them speak. I still stood where I had halted upon the stairs, but they were oblivious to my presence.

'Lucius, my child, Rufus is the leader of this house now and will take care of thee as his cousin.'

'And Marcella?'

I blinked, realizing that was the first time in half a year that Lucius had mentioned me by my Roman name.

'Marcella is Aurelia's property.'

'She deserves her freedom, nonetheless.'

'And if she was free, Lucius, what then? Rufus would have no reason to keep her under this roof and she would be homeless and forsaken in this city.'

Lucius sighed. 'Thou art right, Avia. Yet even Marcella is dependent on thee. Thou and I are the only ones who treat her as an equal. She would be lonely if anything happened to thee.'

'Perhaps so. But I will do my best not to be reckless or put myself in more danger than necessary... I know thou wouldst accompany me if it were not for thy injury.'

'Aye, that is so. And still I wish to go with thee, despite the risk.'

Julia smiled and stroked the face of her grandson. 'I will tell thee of it all when I return. Meanwhile, why dost thou not speak with Marcella?'

'Perhaps, if she will have me. I sometimes doubt whether she wishes me to be there or dreads my presence.'

'She does not, but rather feels the same as thou dost. Speak with her, Lucius. She appreciates thy company, truly.' There was a pause. 'Well, I must go.' She kissed Lucius lightly on his forehead. 'I will be back, if God so wills.'

'Godspeed, Avia,' Lucius murmured in farewell.

I dared not linger a moment longer. I hastened up the stairs in hopes of escaping to my room before my presence was noticed. But it was too late.

'Enid?' I heard Lucius say before I closed my door.

Panting a little, I made my way to my bed and sat down amid the moonlit darkness of my room. Perhaps I should have waited to hear what Lucius would say, but he had already filled me with such confusion that I did not think I could take much more.

A knock sounded at my door, but I remained where I was.

'Enid, please, I need to speak with thee.'

'I am not going to let thee in.' It felt odd, having to raise my voice loud enough for him to hear.

'Of course not. I can speak through the door well enough.'

I stood up and walked to the door, leaning my ear against it. 'What is it?'

'How much didst thou hear of mine and Julia's conversation?'

I hesitated, unsure how he would respond to my answer. 'All of it. Julia had called my name a moment before thou didst approach her.'

There was silence.

'Enid, promise me thou wilt not tell anyone of what thou didst hear. Most of this household is of the Christiani faith, and those that are not are sympathetic. But should any word of that conversation be heard beyond these walls, it could be disastrous.'

'I promise, Lucius. I may not share thy faith, but I am not so foolish as to put thee into danger.'

'I thank thee. Rest well.'

Then he was gone.

I woke early the next morning, at the hour when the sky was still an ashen pearl before the flaming star of day struck life into it. Outside my window, a thin fog lay amidst the buildings and streets, hiding the valleys between the seven hills of Rome beneath a curtain of mist. I shivered in the early morning chill and dressed quickly, tiptoeing down to the kitchens to eat with the other servants before going to Aurelia's room.

No one answered my knock, and as I did not wish to walk in uninvited, I waited in the atrium, my teeth chattering. Moments passed and I heard nothing. As I raised my fist to knock again, I heard an unexpected scuffling.

Stepping away from the door, I peered into the dimness of the atrium, listening intently. 'Is anyone there?' My voice sounded small in the stillness.

'Enid?'

I knew that voice, and my shoulders relaxed—it was no burglar.

Walking a few steps forward, I found Lucius lying on the floor, leaning back against the wall, his crutch beside him. He was wrapped in his army cloak and looked as if he had spent the night huddled in the corner.

'Lucius? What art thou doing here?' I questioned softly, kneeling down beside him.

'What dost thou think I am doing here?'

'Hast thou been here all night?'

'Aye.' He hoisted himself up further into a sitting position, inhaling sharply when his right knee collided with the wall. 'I am yet waiting for Julia's return.'

'What?' My heart leapt into my throat. 'Art thou saying she has not returned?'

Lucius attempted to rise to his feet but failed, he and his crutch clattering helplessly to the floor. I could not begin to imagine the pain it must have cost him, and yet he only moaned softly through clenched teeth.

'Here, let me.' I slid my arms around him, steadying him as he tried again to get to his feet. Reaching down, I picked up his crutch and held it as he transferred his weight onto it.

'I thank thee, Enid.' I could not see his face clearly in the dimness, but I heard the deep shame in his voice.

'What of Julia?'

He sighed. 'She still has not returned home. Perhaps she stayed the night with fellow Christiani.'

'And if not?'

Lucius' eyes flickered up to meet mine, and even in the faint morning light, I could see that they were full of sorrow and fear. 'She is in Christus' hands. Nothing will happen to her apart from His will.'

I could not understand these Christiani. 'How canst thou have hope?'

He smiled, a pained smile. 'Because there is always hope for those who are in Christ.'

'But how?'

'After thou hast attended to Aurelia, and if thou art free, perhaps we can speak more on this subject.'

'What if Julia has still not returned?'

The smile vanished. 'Only time will tell, Enid.' As he walked away, his soldier's cloak rippled with each awkward step.

PART IV

I stand between two worlds
There is no middle ground for me
The tears that fall
Have wanted it all
There is no return for me

CHAPTER XX

MARCELLA, WHAT IS troubling thee?' Aurelia sat on the edge of her bed waiting for me. Rufus still slept, but I entered her room and closed the door behind me softly.

I relit the oil lamps before answering. 'Julia went last night to a meeting of the Christiani. She still has not come home.' Even in my own ears, my voice sounded hollow, as though it was detached from me.

Aurelia's forehead creased together in a worried frown. 'Marcella, thou art certain?'

I closed the lid of the chest, the soft folds of her stola settling over my arm. 'Lucius waited all night in the atrium for her return.'

Aurelia rose and sat down on the chair before the polished bronze mirror as I began to prepare her for the baths. 'Perhaps she is merely staying at one of the other Christiani's homes for the night. After all, it did rain.'

'Perhaps,' I agreed, but my voice was doubtful. Lucius had said the same thing.

'What is this?' Rufus muttered sleepily, blinking against the lamplight.

Aurelia turned to look at him. 'Marcella says that Julia has been out all night. Did she mention she might be staying at one of the Christiani's homes?'

Rufus sat up. 'She did not even tell me she would be going out.' His voice was impassive, but even I could tell that he was worried—and angry. He pushed aside the bedclothes and dressed quickly, leaving us in awkward silence.

I finished tidying Aurelia's hair with shaking hands.

When the midday meal had passed and still Julia had not returned, Rufus set out from the house. Silence reigned in his absence. Aurelia complained of a slight headache and lay down to rest, leaving me free to spend the afternoon as I pleased.

I went to Lucius' room and knocked on the door, listening for an answer. I knew he might still be sleeping after being awake all night, and I also knew my behaviour might be deemed as improper by some, but I did not care. I was concerned for him as well as Julia. If anything was to happen to her, he would have to pay the consequences in some way or another. As would we all.

'Intrabit,' came the response a few moments later.

Glancing around to see whether anyone was watching, I opened the door and slipped inside.

'Oh, Enid, 'tis thee.'

Lucius sat on his bed. He appeared to have just awoken from a deep sleep, for he looked only half awake. 'Has Julia returned yet?'

I shook my head, still leaning against the door. 'Rufus has gone out in search of her, but...' My voice trailed off.

'But what?'

'I fear it will take much more than that to find her.'

'What makes thee say that?' He untangled himself from the enveloping folds of his military cloak. He had not even bothered to take it off before sleeping.

'Many things.'

Lucius looked up and beckoned me to come sit beside him. 'What sort of things?' he prompted.

I sat down next to him and he placed one of the loose edges of his great cloak across my shoulders. It was warm enough in the spring sun, but here indoors, it was quite cold.

'Intuition, for one. And I think she would have returned by now if she had stayed with some other family last night.' When he said nothing, I continued, 'And thee?'

He glanced at me and swallowed. 'Thou art right. I know God does not allow anything to happen to His children that is not according to His plan, yet I also know that many times His plans for us are not what we would wish.'

'Is that thy comfort in this?' My tone held a mix of mockery and curiosity.

Lucius opened his mouth and then closed it before looking me full in the face. 'Aye, but that is not my only comfort. I also know that my God is sovereign and nothing happens that is not part of His will. Unlike the gods of other religions, He does not change with varying circumstances. The world may fall to pieces around us, but He will endure unchanged forever. I know that His promises, likewise, are for all generations, and even if Julia were to perish among the other thousands of Christiani martyrs, she would go home to live forever with her Saviour—as will I, when I die.'

I stared at him in wonder at his conviction and passion. 'What makes thee so sure of this?'

He smiled, a distant look in his eyes as if he could see things, pleasant things, that I could not. 'Because I know it to be true,' he said softly, with depth of feeling. 'Why else dost thou hear of Christiani dying with a song on their lips, peacefully reconciled to the fate before them? And in my own heart, I know that it is true.'

Silence fell between us—an awkward silence, on my part. In one sense, I understood Lucius' comfort; yet I did not share it, and that made me afraid. I did not have peace about whatever my future would be. I was frightened of the uncertainty, the frailty of it all. And yet, I did not feel ready to submit myself to the God of the Christiani.

I wondered if I would ever be.

Rufus did not return home until late that evening when *cena* was being cleared away. At the sight of his dejected look, the smile on Lucius' face faded and Aurelia drew in her breath sharply. A stab of cold fear went through me.

'Oh, Rufus, what is it?' Aurelia asked.

He did not answer for some time, but simply stood there in the doorway, the torchlight casting his flickering silhouette into the peristylium beyond.

'There is nothing that can be done.' His voice was thick with emotion. He strode forward and sat down on the marble slabs that served as dining couches.

'What happened? Where is Julia?' Aurelia would not relent. Indeed, she spoke for us all.

'Somewhere in the Hypogeum, that is all I know.'

My blood froze. I had often heard of—though I had never seen—the Hypogeum, the subterranean chamber beneath the Colosseum where the beasts and gladiators were kept for the Games.

Aurelia wailed, rising to her feet and swaying where she stood. 'Is there no hope?'

I went to her and put an arm around her to keep her from collapsing.

Rufus grew irritated. 'I have tried every possible thing in my power to free her. There is nothing more I can do.' He got to his feet and left without another word. I could hardly blame him for his wrathful outburst.

Unfortunately, Aurelia was less resilient than I, and I had to escort her to her room, undress her, and put her to bed, all the while listening to her weep and fret about what would happen to Julia, its effects on Rufus, and what it might entail for them all until I nearly lost my patience. Yet she rested quietly at last, and I slipped out into the chilly spring twilight of the peristylium.

'Surely there is some way—' Lucius' voice broke the silence.

I froze in my steps and listened.

'Nay, Lucius,' Rufus interrupted his cousin. ''Tis impossible. The Hypogeum is heavily guarded. We would only join her in prison.' He sighed heavily. 'I know, I know. But what can I— what can we do? Nothing.'

'I know those prisons. Augustus and I guarded them during our military training. It may yet work.'

'It is too much of a risk! Why canst thou not get that into thine head?' Rufus smashed his fist against a pillar and swore at the pain. I jumped at his exclamation, the empty pottery cup in my hand falling to the ground and shattering.

'Who's there?' Rufus called out anxiously.

'Marcella.' The word fell trembling from my mouth. I heard someone sigh in relief.

'Marcella, come here.' It was Lucius, his voice gently caressing my name. I almost did not mind that he called me by my Roman appellation.

I drew near to them until I stood by Lucius' side. His fingers reached out and drew my hand into his, and I no longer felt the cold as keenly. 'Art thou speaking of helping Julia escape?' I asked softly, lest anyone should hear from the shadows.

'Lucius believes it possible, but I see no use in it,' Rufus said simply.

Lucius' jaw tightened. 'I will not stop until I have tried everything possible.'

'And what canst thou do?'

I felt Lucius' embarrassment in the pause that followed.

Rufus ran a hand over his face. 'I—I am sorry, cousin. That was cruel of me to say. Forgive me, please.'

'I do,' Lucius murmured, but he still gripped my hand tightly.

'Can not Rufus and I do it, if thou tellest us what to do?' I spoke up.

'Marcella, 'tis useless,' Rufus objected.

My blood boiled. 'We can at least try!'

'We would have to get past the watch,' Rufus protested. 'I have the senate's approval to move after evening curfew without being seized by the guard, but what of Marcella? And that is before we even get to the gates! Many Christiani are being held there, not Julia alone. The guard will be doubled. Lucius, 'tis impossible.'

'Rufus, wilt thou at least listen to my plan? If only for Julia's sake and not mine?' Lucius pleaded.

The torchlight flickered behind us in the atrium, leaving the peristylium bathed in a fitful glow from the moon. The tension rose in my own heart as I watched the two of them. If Rufus agreed to Lucius' plan, would it succeed? Would it all come to nothing—or worse, would we end up facing the same fate as Julia?

Rufus sighed heavily. 'All right. But if it is too dangerous, I will risk neither my life nor Marcella's in a useless cause that will only end in our death. What is thy plan?'

Half an hour later, Rufus and I stepped out into the evening air, the dampness enveloping my feet where the edges of the woolen cloak I had borrowed from Lucius failed to reach. Sounds came muffled through the hood, which hid my crimson hair, and I had to watch Rufus closely so as not to lose him in the streets while we made our way silently down to the Hypogeum.

Fear and hope warred in my mind, and I wondered if our mad venture could possibly succeed. It reminded me oddly of the games my brothers and I played when we were bairns, especially deer-and-hunters—one child quietly sneaking through the village and forest, the rest of us tracking and chasing him down. But in this game, Rufus and I were the hunted and not the hunters. The thought filled me with dread.

We halted a street away from the Hypogeum, having walked unseen until now, and waited as the guard slipped past our hiding place in the shadows. My heart raced and I gasped for air. How I wished Lucius was by my side! But his crippled leg would only hinder us.

'Marcella, art thou ready?' Rufus' hushed voice broke into my thoughts.

I nodded, shivering. 'Aye,' I forced out. There was no time to worry about what could go wrong. There was only time to act.

We dashed across the street, the sound of our sandals slapping against the pavement abnormally loud in my ears. My heart was in my throat, and my throat was terribly dry. A public fountain stood nearby, the water bubbling merrily into the small pool below the spout. I glanced at it, licking my chapped lips, and looked at Rufus. I opened my mouth to ask if I could run the short distance and quench my thirst, but he motioned for me to come closer.

'On the count of three, thou must run across the street and hide in the shadows of the arches, away from the torchlight. Understand?'

'Aye.' My palms were sweaty and I wiped them on my tunic. Thunder rumbled in the distance. The moon was hidden by clouds.

'*Unus, duo, tres.*'

A moment later, I was safely hidden from sight, my breath coming in ragged gasps. I was no longer used to exertion of this sort. Rufus joined me, his cloak billowing behind him in the rain. I felt his breath hot against the side of my face and I peered around the corner, seeing only the smoking brazier.

'What now?' I ventured to ask, then I froze as if turned into a marble statue.

Rufus cursed under his breath.

CHAPTER XXI

WITHIN MOMENTS, THE patrol marching around the building would pass directly in front of our hiding place and the light of their torches would most assuredly find us. If I had been nervous before, I was more so now. I thought my heart would burst from beating so fast.

If we were found out, I doubted that any excuses would free us from sharing Julia's fate. Sympathy for the Christiani was prohibited; we would be shown no mercy. Like as not, we would be thrown into a cell and fed to the wild beasts as breakfast in the Colosseum along with the rest of the prisoners.

'Marcella, I need thee to follow me and not say a word,' Rufus hissed before stepping out of the shadows and walking where the guards would soon come, his pace fast and firm.

I followed him, my fingers tingling in fright. What was he doing?

A moment later, he broke into a run and dashed across the street, vanishing in the shadows of a building beyond. Without further hesitation, I ran after him. My hood fell back, rain pelting me in the face.

Once there, we watched with gasping breath as the guard rounded the corner and continued marching around the Hypogeum, their torches smoking and hissing in the rain. I felt sick with nervousness and swallowed hard. We had come too close to being discovered, far too close for my liking and, I think, also for Rufus'.

'They have a doubled guard at the entrances and another encircling the premises,' Rufus whispered hoarsely, his eyes roving constantly in search of danger. ''Tis naught but madness if we try to free her. Even Lucius would see that, were he here. We must go back before we are caught.'

'As thou wishest,' I murmured, my heart sinking to the soles of my feet. We had been Julia's last hope of rescue.

Neither Rufus nor I spoke another word until we returned to the Caelian Hill, the rain slowly soaking through our clothes. Lucius' military cloak was of thick wool, so I was only slightly damp, but Rufus was less fortunate. There was no thunder now, only rain, a misty curtain that fell unceasingly from the heavens and ran in rivulets down the streets.

Once inside the atrium, which was quiet save for the pattering of raindrops in the pool, I slipped back my hood and bade Rufus goodnight. He did not respond—perhaps he did not hear me—and went to his room, leaving me alone in the damp darkness.

I took off the cloak and laid it on one of the benches in the atrium before stepping into the next room. I did not know if Lucius had retired for the night, but I thought it unlikely he would sleep until he knew if our mission had succeeded.

Braziers burned among the columns, the overhanging roof protecting the flames from the water pouring down from the black skies. The peristylium appeared empty, for I heard no one, and the shadows remained undisturbed.

'Lucius?' I spoke into the peaceful silence of the night, stepping carefully in the darkness lest I trip over some unseen object. 'Lucius, art thou there?'

Silence met my words, and I had nearly decided to retire for the night when I heard a response at last. 'Aye, Enid.'

I followed the source of the voice until I stood next to Lucius. He was leaning his right shoulder against a column, staring at the shadows of the gardens. I touched his hand lightly and he looked at me, slipping his free arm across my shoulders. I leaned against him, the heightened sense of danger from the narrow escape fading away, leaving me utterly exhausted. I minded then how cold I had become, standing in the Aprilis night dressed only in my thin slave's tunic. I should have kept the cloak for warmth.

We stood quietly, listening to the rain, until at last I dared to ask, 'What now?'

He hesitated before answering. 'Pray for grace.'

'Grace?' I was bewildered by his response.

'Aye. Grace for Julia, that she might endure whatever is to befall her. Grace for those who in their own ignorance suppress the truth and murder so many of God's children, that they might be saved before it is too late. And grace for us, that if the worst should come, we might brave the loss and hold fast in the storm that is surely to come.' He looked at me again, but I could not see the details of his face in the darkness. 'And thou? What wilt thou do?'

'I do not know. Thy faith is not mine.' My words sounded as hopeless as I felt.

If Julia was God's child, as she claimed to be, would He not have allowed us to rescue her? And yet He did not. Perhaps He was as weak as any other god, though something in the firm, trusting way Lucius and Julia believed in Him made me wish to think otherwise.

Lucius gently caressed my shoulders, a ripple of warmth fluttering in my chest as he did so. 'I have not ceased to pray for thee, nor given up hope,' he replied tenderly.

'I am still afraid to trust,' I murmured.

'While there is life, there is hope.'

I was silent for several moments, thinking about what he said. 'Is there hope for Julia?'

Lucius sighed. 'Rufus spoke to me earlier, before thou came to us…he had even appealed to the Emperor for her release on grounds that she was forced to be a partaker of the Christiani's rituals. But Domitian has no pity, no mercy…. It is in my heart that we will be witnesses to her death in the Colosseum before many more days pass.'

The warmth I felt at being so near him fled at this news, the cold hand of fear taking its place. 'So soon?'

He did not answer and it was then that I realized that tears were flowing down his face. When he did speak, it was in broken phrases, and his voice cracked at the edges. 'I never knew my father. He—he died fighting against Boudicca's rebellion before I was born. My mother brought me up in Halwyn's home—he was a friend of my father's—until I was about seven years old. Then Halwyn and his family could no longer keep us under their roof. My mother sent word to my great-uncle, Gaius Suetonius Paulinus, the one who led the counterattack on Boudicca's forces, saying that I was his great-nephew. H-he rejected me on grounds that I was illegitimate and sent me with my mother to his sister, Julia. She was very kind to us, but'—he drew in a shuddering sigh—'it was hard on me and even more so on my mother. She died a few months after our arrival in Rome. And then I was even more alone than before.' He broke off abruptly, a few gasping sobs escaping from his lips. 'Wherever I went, those who knew me—who knew of my heritage—mocked me. I was belittled and cursed…Julia was the only one who was kind to me. If not for her nurture and care, I do not know where I would be. Probably drowned in the Tiber out of hopelessness and self-loathing. I owe her so much, and yet…and yet I have never been able to repay her.' He inhaled sharply, his breath trembling. 'And now she is going to die and there is nothing I, nor anyone else, can do for her.'

I was silent, tears slipping down my cheeks. I longed to alleviate his grief, but there was nothing I could possibly do.

'There were times,' he continued after regaining his composure somewhat, 'when I was young in the faith, that I thought—I wondered—what I would do if something like this happened.' He shrugged, his arm across my shoulders moving slightly. 'I always thought that it would be hard to continue living if I lost her. It was hard enough to go on after my mother died. I know that God will provide solace, but it is still so difficult.'

He exhaled softly and when he spoke again, his voice was under control once more. 'And yet, He has blessed me beyond all I could ask for.' His tone became unspeakably gentle and I could almost hear the smile on his lips. 'He gave me thee.'

The tenderness in his voice sent a thrill through my being and I stared up at him, astonished. Was Lucius truly saying what I thought he was? 'What dost thou mean?'

He leaned against the column for support and put both of his hands on my shoulders. 'In the midst of my pain and loneliness of never belonging, God gave me thee, a light and hope in my life.'

My heart began to race and I found myself strangely short of breath. This could not be happening, could it? 'Lucius, thou dost not know what thou sayest! It can never be—I am a slave, thou art free…I am not of the Christiani.' I could scarcely believe what I was hearing.

'Shh.' He laid a finger on my lips. 'Enid, I yet pray for thee. And thou wert never a slave in Britannia. Thou and I are equals in everything but faith.'

'And that difference in itself is great.' I did not want to believe and then be disappointed, as I had been when the Romans tore me away from Telyn. My love had been thwarted before; I could not bear it if it happened again.

'Oh, Enid! I will not give up hope.'

'Why not?' I was so afraid to believe this was happening, so afraid of waking up and finding it a dream fashioned out of my exhausted mind....

'Because I love thee!' His words rang in my head, even though he spoke softly.

My heart stopped beating and I gazed at him in silence. *He loves me?*

All I had hoped for, all I had dreamed of, all I had convinced myself would never happen had happened, leaving me helpless in wonder and astonishment. 'Truly?' I whispered breathlessly, unable to manage anything more.

'Aye, my lovely Enid, *dw i'n caru chdi.*' And then his lips met my own.

Until that moment, I had not known what immortality tasted like. The exhaustion and horror of the evening, my bitterness and hatred of my slavery, my fears for the unknown future, and my confusion and pain melted away into weightless bliss. I was as light as the clouds of heaven—if Lucius had not been holding me in his arms, I might have floated away altogether.

And then the weightlessness was washed away as my senses were flooded with love and warmth and depth of passion. We were no longer Briton and Roman, no longer slave and outcast; the distance between us vanished and we met as one complete being. I no longer heard the rain nor saw the darkness; there was only him and me, forever.

I had always imagined what it might feel like to be kissed, but imagination fell utterly short of the magical reality of loving and being loved in return. I was not imagining this—it was real, beautifully real, and I did not want it to end.

When Lucius pulled back at last, he said softly, "'Tis late. Many things will happen on the morrow and it is best we prepare for them with a good night's sleep. Rest well, *fy nghariad*.' He bowed his head, took up his crutch, and went to his room, leaving me in silence, but there was a lightness in his step that had not been there before.

My mind was whirling. I could hardly fathom all that had taken place over the last two days. My heart still pounded in uncontrolled ecstasy as I closed my eyes, reliving Lucius' words and what had followed after.

My elation soon faded away into remorse as I retired for the night. What was to be done? I knew Lucius found comfort in the promises of his God, and I supposed Julia did as well, but what of me? Was I willing to risk everything I had built my hopes on—to surrender it all in reckless abandon to Someone whose followers were daily hunted down and executed? Was it worth it? Lucius claimed it was, as did Julia. And now Julia was to pay the price.

These thoughts echoed in my mind until at last I fell into a dreamless sleep, too exhausted to make further sense of them. I needed my rest, even as Lucius had said.

For who knew what tomorrow would bring.

CHAPTER XXII

THE NEXT MORNING dawned grey and cheerless. I had thought there would be a trial for Julia and the others, but when we gathered in the atrium at Rufus' bidding, he told us that she was to be put to death that day along with the other Christiani in the Colosseum. I had never attended the Games myself, being a slave and having no interest in that form of entertainment, but this time was different. This was to be the death of someone who had shown great kindness to me—whom I loved. I wanted to go, if only to see her one last time—and to be there for Lucius, whom I knew would grieve her death harder than the rest of us.

Rufus, Aurelia, Lucius, and I, as well as a few accompanying attendants, set off in silence for the infamous Colosseum. There were many others also heading for the same place that morning, but they were laughing and boisterous. After all, they were not to be witnesses to the death of a loved one.

The Colosseum was beyond my comprehension, not only in size but in noise. The cacophony of fifty thousand people all talking at once was deafening; I was quickly overwhelmed and longed to return to the relative quiet of the Septimius villa. I slipped my hand in Lucius' and clung to him like a drowning man, afraid of being separated from him by the crushing mass of people. Nothing in all my life had prepared me for this, let alone what was to take place.

We were seated on the lower rows of the immense structure, as Rufus was an assistant to one of the senators and therefore granted the privilege of being nearer to the action in the arena. However, as the sun broke through the dense, grey clouds and rose higher in the sky, the people in the top rows were shaded while we were left to sweat in the growing heat of the day.

Lucius squeezed my hand gently. The sound around us was dying to a mere buzz, like the monotonous humming of a thousand bees. Hard to our left, a handful of the Praetorian guard, clad in purple and black, stationed themselves in the Emperor's box. Trumpeters came out, their instruments gleaming in the sun, and heralded the coming of Emperor Domitian and his entourage. I could hardly see their faces for the distance, only the bright and flashy colours of their clothing.

'What is happening?' I heard myself say to Lucius.

'I think the Emperor is going to make a speech—or one of his men will. That is the custom before the Games begin.'

'Art thou afraid?' I asked a moment later, looking up at him as the pale grey sunlight cast a strange hue on his blue-black hair.

He turned to me, his green-gold eyes glistening with tears. 'Afraid for myself? Nay. I only wish to be strong for her when the time comes. I pray that she holds firm until the end and that she will feel no pain.' His voice was soft, a sharp contrast to the commotion around us.

Like the rolling of a great wave onto a beach, the crowd's clamor rose throughout the amphitheatre, the roar erupting into cheers and shouts. One of the many gates on the floor of the Colosseum opened, its yawning mouth leading into empty darkness. The crowd clapped their hands in delight as a group of men and women were led out into the center, their hands bound.

Bile rose in my throat and I swallowed it down with great difficulty. What was going to happen?

'Is Julia there?' I tried to make myself heard above the discord around us.

'I think not, but it is a great distance.' He leaned in closer as if to get a better view. 'Nay, I do not believe she is among them.'

The Emperor stood and raised his hand for silence. When a substantial quiet lay among the masses, he said, 'Welcome, *populi!*'

'How can we hear his voice so well?' I nudged Lucius with my elbow.

'The structure was designed that way. Anyone in the center—or especially where the emperor sits—can say anything and be heard clearly by everyone else,' he responded before Domitian began to speak again.

'Behold, the Christiani before thee! They stand guilty of the crimes with which we have become well acquainted these many years, yet when offered a chance to repent of their outrages against the Roman Empire, they continue in their errors! Therefore, they must be punished, lest they breed corruption and harm and rebellion against the Emperor, against Rome, against Roman citizens!' Domitian did not even try to keep the mockery out of his voice. 'Watch now their rightful demise, the just punishment for their atrocities committed against Rome and her people!' He sat down again as the crowd booed at the small group of quite ordinary men and women standing meekly silent in the center of the sandy arena.

'This is so wrong,' I whispered to Lucius, my voice trembling in anger. 'They have done nothing that is against Roman law!'

'Aye, and I pray that one day God will make it plain.' He spoke quietly, like the spring breeze peacefully blowing among the branches of the almond tree in the peristylium.

Then the guards surrounding the Christiani left them to suffer their fate, and I could but watch in mute horror at what followed.

Hidden trapdoors beneath the sand of the Colosseum dropped down and several lions leapt up into the arena, the audience screaming and shouting in excitement. Yet the Christiani remained unmoved—as if unafraid, though I could not understand how they could face their death without fear.

A strange sound filled the air: no roaring of lions or tearing of flesh, no screaming or crying. It was *singing*. I blinked, dumbfounded. What sort of madness possessed these people that they would be so calm as to sing before they died? Was it truly their belief in their God? What sort of God gave His followers such peace when staring into the jaws of pain and death? I was not the only person amazed, for the roar of the crowd hushed, whether from shock or respect I could not say.

Yet the lions were neither as patient nor as respectful as the crowd. Snarls escaped their fanged mouths. They circled their prey, paws padding on the fresh sand as the audience waited with bated breath for the attack.

Once they sprung, the singing dissipated into a pandemonium of painful screams. The crowd watched the spectacle in a frenzied bloodlust, as if the slaughter of innocent human beings had no effect on their conscience. My stomach, however, turned inside out in disgust and horror and I closed my eyes as the only escape left to me. But there was no escaping from the sound.

'When will it end?' I moaned to no one in particular.

Lucius did not reply, and I opened my eyes to see him looking down at his feet, his jaw clenched tightly. 'Who knows?' he said bitterly, his voice betraying his abhorrence.

I do not know how long the slaughter lasted, for I did not look up again until the cheering stopped. A listless quiet took its place as the lions were secured in their cages, the brutally mutilated remains of the Christiani taken out, and clean sand sprinkled over the blood.

A large wooden pole set up on a wagon was brought out next and left in the center of the area. Chills crept up my spine and I tightened my grip on Lucius' hand. How I wished this horrible reality was only a dream and Julia safe from harm!

The Emperor stood, his speech brief and terribly heart-wrenching to the few of us seated there awaiting the death of someone we loved. 'Not only do numbers of the Christiani flood the lower classes, but they also exist among the ranks of the patricians! Behold, the sister of one of our renowned generals—watch her succumb to the same fate as her *brothers* and *sisters*, who are no more than slaves and servants!'

I loathed Domitian and detested his sneering tones. It was not right.

Julia did not deserve this.

My mental tirade was interrupted by the gates being opened once more, this time to reveal the victim, her arms held captive by the guards on either side. She was dressed in a flimsy gown, a mockery of modesty, but it was better than nothing—most Christiani were executed naked, or so I had heard. Her hair hung tangled and loose down to her waist, a dirtied white-gold curtain, but her face was serene and betrayed no fear. They tied her to the post in the center of the arena, facing the Emperor, and I could see her face no longer.

Lucius inhaled sharply and I suddenly worried that he might cause a scene and thereby doom us all, but he remained seated, clutching my hand as if by doing so he could somehow stay the madness.

'Julia Maxima, I ask thee one last time, wilt thou recant thy beliefs in thy God?' Even now, they were sneering at her. The mockery caused my blood to boil, driving away my tears. 'Even now, the Emperor's mercy extends to thee if thou wilt but say, "Death to the Christiani's God."'

A complete silence followed as everyone waited with bated breath for the outcome. I longed for Julia to say it, if only that she might be returned safely back to us, and yet I did not wish her to betray her faith. If she did, then there was no hope in the world—no hope at all.

A cold sweat broke out on my brow as I looked from the pale figure tied to the pole to the purple-clad Emperor in his box and back again.

Julia responded at last, her voice clear and confident, ringing out in the waiting silence of the Colosseum. 'Death, death to all the gods! Death to the unbelief that festers in thy hearts! Death to the fear and uncertainty and hopelessness of a life apart from the Christiani's God! Death to Satan and all his demonic hosts which even now hold thy souls in their sway!' I strained my ears to hear what she said next above the screaming crowd jumping to their feet in anger at her words. 'Blessed be Christus for giving us eternal life and peace with Him forever!'

I gasped and looked at Lucius, who was staring at his avia, tears streaming down his cheeks.

The guards stepped forward and, with one deft movement, tore the garment Julia was wearing before leaving the arena.

Another gate opened and a wild bear was let loose.

Tears spilled down my face now, tears of anger and tears of grief.

Then I heard it—Julia's voice raised in song. I knew that song, for she had often sung it to me when I was sick and later recovering. The words were from the letter she loved, written to the Romans by the Apostle they called Paul.

'*What shall we then say to these things? If God be for us, who can be against us?*

'*Who shall separate us from the love of Christ? shall tribulation, or distress, or persecution, or famine, or nakedness, or peril, or sword? As it is written, For Thy sake we are killed all the day long; we are accounted as sheep for the slaughter.*

'*Nay, in all these things we are more than conquerors through Him that loved us.*

'*For I am persuaded, that neither death, nor life, nor angels, nor principalities, nor powers, nor things present, nor things to come, nor height, nor depth, nor any other creature, shall be able to separate us from the love of God, which is in Christ Jesus our Lord....*'

I do not think she finished the song, but even if she did, the words were lost in the cries of the crowd and the growls of the starved and angry bear. I could not stand to watch, but buried my face in Lucius' shoulder as I wept for the sheer lunacy of it all.

He slipped his arm around me and leaned his head on mine, saying nothing while his tears ran down and mingled with my own. I longed to escape this terrible place, but I could not. If anything, it would draw unwanted attention. So I stayed, clinging to Lucius as my only anchor in that moment of uncontrollable grief.

When the sound died down at last, I looked up through blinding tears. The bear was being caged and the servants who worked at the Colosseum sprinkled sand on the martyred blood that hallowed the ground where so many had died before.

Julia had not deserved such a death.

'Let us go. Aurelia has swooned,' Rufus said, leaning over the pair of us.

It was a good excuse, even if it was true, and we departed, leaving that place of bloodthirsty hysteria behind us. The streets, while not entirely empty, were a welcome quiet after the chaos of the amphitheatre.

As we returned home, my mind was awhirl. Julia's God had not saved her from death, but she had died in such peace. Surely, if death was inevitable, that peace would be invaluable. I had seen it evidenced not only in her life, but also in Lucius', so I knew it to be true and not merely a façade that she had managed to uphold until her death. I had seen that peace under trial, and her God had not failed her. Nothing more was holding me back from surrendering myself to her God save my stubborn pride.

The peaceful silence of the Septimius villa was a refreshing change and I heaved a sigh of relief once we were safe behind its doors. After attending to Aurelia, I returned to Rufus and Lucius, who stood in the atrium speaking to each other in low tones.

'So what now? Surely they will make an investigation here?' Lucius was saying.

'I do not know,' Rufus replied gravely. 'Perhaps they will let us be. But methinks thou art safer elsewhere.'

'Where would I go? There is no place that would accept me—thou knowest this.' Lucius sighed. 'These are dangerous times for us—I, by sharing in Julia's faith, and thou, by being associated with us both. And I would play the coward by fleeing.'

'Lucius, 'tis not cowardice. Perhaps thou might even bear the tidings of thy gospel to peoples elsewhere who have not yet heard it. Would that be considered cowardice?'

Lucius shook his dark head gently. 'Nay, I suppose not. I will give it thought.'

'Meanwhile, look out for Marcella. Aurelia spoke to me this morning about the possibility of giving her freedom. If that be so, then thou art all she will have left.' Rufus nodded in my direction and left in silence.

Lucius turned, seeing me for the first time. 'Enid, what is it?' His tone was gentle, yet terribly sad. There were still traces of tears on his cheeks, but he was trying to be brave in spite of it, even as we all were.

I stepped towards him, inhaling deeply. 'I wish to become one of the Christiani.'

CHAPTER XXIII

THE FOLLOWING DAYS were ones of great uncertainty, and yet they were filled with peace. The future was as clear as the thick fog that sometimes rolled in from the sea and covered the valleys of my homeland, but I rested in the comfort of the promises of the Christiani's God, who was now my own. At any moment, the Imperial Guard could knock on the doors and take us all away to our deaths—and yet I was no longer afraid of them as I had been. Lucius and I were both blessed with a quiet tranquility during that time of grief and doubt.

That said, I continued to have some apprehension about the future. I knew now that whatever happened was God's will—an assurance I had lacked before—but I still wondered what would happen to me, to Lucius, to all of us. My dreams, insignificant as they were, had begun to come true at last, and I feared they would be destroyed before they would ever be fully realized.

Trust. It was something I was not much acquainted with, but I had to learn it. I had to learn to trust and depend on the God of the Christiani in a way I had never trusted anyone before. It was the only way I could go on—that any of us could go on. When life strips away everything familiar, what else can one do?

Aurelia noticed the change in me, from constant worry to newfound peace, but she only mentioned it once, saying that she was glad I seemed happy. Indeed, the day after Julia's martyrdom, she called me to Rufus' study before the midday meal, just when my help was needed most in the kitchens. I could not disobey, so I left the chaotic bustle of the culinae and entered the contemplative calm of the tablinum, relishing the quiet atmosphere of books and quills and ink.

'Marcella, dost thou know why thou art here?' Aurelia began. She stood beside her husband, who was seated before the ivory enameled desk, and they both watched me, noting my every movement.

'Nay, I do not,' I replied simply, clasping my hands behind me. The sun came through the curtained hanging that partitioned the room off from the rest of the house, the muted rays falling upon my back with comforting warmth.

Aurelia took her hand off her husband's shoulder and stepped towards me. 'Since Julia's death yesterday, I have been brought to a reckoning with the brevity of life.' She paused a long while before continuing. 'Thou has served me well these five years. But I think thou still desirest thy freedom, nonetheless.'

I opened my mouth to reply, but she was not finished.

'Last night, I could not sleep, so I woke Rufus and discussed the matter with him. As he has had to study the law as part of his training for holding Roman office, he was able to write out this document.' She took up a rolled parchment in her hands and handed it to me. ''Tis not a formal manumission, as that would take time in the courts—but I am thinking it will do well enough.'

I took it from her, still bewildered by her unusual solemnity. Breaking the seal, I unrolled it and hastily scanned its contents. I looked up, unable to believe what was happening. 'Thou art giving me my freedom—truly?'

'Aye, thou hast earned it well.' Aurelia smiled kindly and I realized then how much she had grown up in the past few days. In the place of the young girl I had known was a woman, mature in the face of death. The girlish twinkle had not left her eyes, but there was alongside it the seriousness that comes with age.

'Mind, 'tis not a formal manumission.' Rufus unclasped his hands and leaned back. 'So thou wilt not have the privileges of a Roman citizen. But neither does Lucius, due to the circumstances surrounding his birth, and he lives life well enough despite that.'

'I do not think I would much like being a Roman citizen anyway.' A wry smile played on my lips.

'That is what I thought,' Rufus replied, a boyish grin on his face.

I read the document through once more in silence, the reality sinking in slowly. My chest tightened and I clutched the parchment as if it was the physical manifestation of my dreams. After spending so long dreaming and wishing for it to happen, I was free. I had longed for this since the day the slave traders took me captive, since those long hours of suffering in the slave ship's hold, since my failed escape and the whipping that followed. All my bitterness and hatred against the Romans was gone. Joy coursed through my veins at the thought. I was free—truly free.

I looked up, suddenly remembering that Aurelia and Rufus were there, and said, 'I thank thee,' before bowing my head out of habit and leaving the room, the parchment springing back up into its rolled position.

'Oh, Marcella!' Aurelia's voice stopped me, and I glanced over my shoulder at her. 'Rufus and I both know that thou hast no place to go, so thou art welcome to stay here as long as thou needest.'

'I thank thee.' I smiled. 'Thou art both very kind to me.'

I stepped out into the spring sunshine and squinted in the sudden brightness. Lucius sat in the peristylium, bent over some wax tablets in his lap.

'Lucius!' I ran to him, the warm grass tickling my feet.

He looked up, a slight smile appearing on his face. He gestured for me to sit beside him and I did so, seating myself on his left side so that his crippled leg would not lay between us, for I knew that the mere sight of it pained him. 'Tell me, Enid, what brings such a smile to thy face? I have never seen thee smile so—thou shouldst do it more often.'

I flushed with pleasure. 'Aurelia has given me my freedom.' I watched his face, waiting for some sort of expression of surprise to appear, but it did not, much to my disappointment.

'Ah, I see. Well, I am very happy for thee.' His voice was unusually stiff and distant, and a tingle of fear chilled my spine.

I laid my hand on the marble bench, the warm white stone heated by the sun. 'Lucius, what is it?'

He shook his head. 'Nothing of importance.' He folded together the hinged wax tablets and laid them aside. 'So, thou art no longer a slave?' He smiled at me again, but his eyes were guarded, as if something else was on his mind other than my freedom.

'Aye, I am completely free.' I wondered if he would understand my meaning, but it felt forced. He was keeping something from me.

'I am glad for thee, Enid.'

I tried to smile again, but found I could not. 'Lucius…'

'Aye, Enid, what is it?'

'What wert thou looking at when I came?' I said at last.

'Nothing of importance, as I said before. It will probably all come to nothing, so it does not matter in the end.' He planted a soft kiss on my forehead. 'Now what wilt thou do as thou art no longer Aurelia's slave?'

I was not convinced by his answer, but I decided not to push the matter further. 'I do not know. There is not much of a future for me here, but where else would I go?' I glanced up at him, wondering if he would ask the question that I was waiting for him to ask, but he was staring at the ground, his dark brows drawn together.

He opened his mouth to speak, but the words never came.

'Marcella, I would like to have another word with thee, if thou art willing,' Aurelia called from the far doorway.

I rose to my feet, confused by Lucius' strange behaviour. 'Aye, Aurelia, what is it?' I asked once I stood before her.

'Well, I know thou hast few clothes besides thy slave's tunic, so I wished to tell thee that if thou dost not mind, I will give thee some of mine for thine own use.'

'I thank thee, Aurelia.'

She smiled. 'Thou art welcome, Marcella—or shouldst I call thee Enid? That seems to be Lucius' name for thee.'

I smiled—a small one, but a smile nonetheless. 'Enid is my British name, that is why.' It felt odd to finally tell Aurelia something I had refused to share for so long, but I no longer cared if she knew it. I had forgiven the Romans for what they had done to me—I was free of both hatred and slavery.

'Well then, Enid, I bid thee farewell for now.' She turned and left me in the cool shadows among the columns bordering the peristylium.

I returned to where I had been seated beside Lucius, but he was no longer there. I doubted he wished to speak to me anyway; he had not seemed eager to converse with me a moment ago.

Why was he so reluctant to talk to me? What had he been reading in those tablets? And what was he going to tell me before Aurelia interrupted?

I shook my head. I was not going to magically receive answers to these questions on my own. I rose and returned to my room, shutting the door firmly behind me.

I was still new to the Christiani faith, but one thing I had already begun to put to use was the ability to freely approach God in prayer, whatever it might be about. The worries somehow lessened when I spoke of them to the God Who had redeemed me as His child and Who loved and cared for me more than anyone else ever could.

When I had finished praying, I opened my eyes and heard a knocking on the door. 'Intrabit,' I called, wondering if it was Lucius.

It was Aurelia. In her hands, she carried several garments which I recognized immediately. 'These are for thy permanent use,' she said by way of explanation and laid them on my bed.

'Thou didst not need to give me so many!'

'Nay, 'tis the least I can do. Please let me know if thou needest anything more.'

'I will.'

How many times had I looked in envy at Aurelia's garments and longed for them to be my own instead of the shameful slave tunic? And now, they were mine. I could hardly wrap my mind around it.

Aurelia lingered. 'Has Lucius spoken to thee?'

I paused. 'What dost thou mean?'

Aurelia sighed. 'Perhaps 'tis nothing. Only I have noticed Rufus and him speaking oft together in whispered tones when they think I am not there. I wondered if thou knew what it was about.'

I understood immediately. 'I would not know. Whatever it is, Lucius is keeping it a secret from me also.'

Aurelia nodded. 'Well, I must not keep thee. Oh!' She halted and reentered my room, placing something cold and metallic in my hands. 'I wish thee to have this. It matches thy eyes well.' She smiled, a twinkle in her soft, dark eyes, and left before I could give it back, closing the door behind her.

I looked down into my palm and saw the silver-and-emerald necklace she had let me borrow when I was disguised as her companion the first time we visited this house. I held it around my neck and looked into the simple piece of polished bronze to catch a murky reflection. I could finally see its beauty without regret, for I was free and no longer forbidden to wear such costly things. Less than a year ago, I had hated the sight of it. So much had happened since then.

I sat down on the bed and fingered the jewelry in my hands. So much had happened, aye, and so much had changed. If I could have seen on that day how much could change in such a short time, would I have had the courage to go on? Would any of us? Was that why we were forbidden to see into the future? Perhaps that was why life happened in individual days, each one seeming so mundane and yet yielding to the whole, revealing years and events across the course of history, from the dawn of Time until its ending…

A sudden clattering from the kitchens reminded me that it was time for the midday meal. Saving my thoughts for another time, I rose and went down, leaving the necklace on my bed, the sunlight glimmering in the dark green depths of the jewels.

That night, after *cena* was over—I still ate in the kitchens, not yet ready for my life to change completely from that of a slave to that of a free woman—I returned to my room and put Aurelia's things in a small chest, saving a plain white stola to wear instead of my slave's tunic. I had just finished changing when I heard a knock on my door.

'Aye, what is it?' I asked, adjusting the folds of my stola.

'Enid, I have a favor to ask of thee.' It was Lucius.

I opened the door quickly and looked into his startled face. 'What is it?' I questioned again, curious.

'Wilt thou come with me?'

'Where?' I asked, confused.

'To the peristylium. I have a few questions to ask thee, and 'twould be unseemly to be found in thy room.'

My face flushed in embarrassment at my eagerness. 'Aye, I will come down.'

A few moments later, I joined him on one of the benches. The sun was setting and the dying colours were displayed across the sky above us like some bloodied banner of victory. Slaves were lighting the braziers to provide more light, but all else was quiet. Lucius did not speak until they were gone.

'Enid,' he said softly. 'Dost thou remember those talks with Julia about our faith?'

'Of course,' I replied. 'How could I forget?'

He laughed and I smiled awkwardly, unsure of what he was laughing at. 'Enid, thou soundest so serious.' The laughter ceased. 'Nay, but I had a reason. Dost thou remember her speaking of baptism?'

'Is that why thou hast been so secretive of late?'

'That is not the only reason.' He sighed. 'I know 'tis very soon since thy conversion and most wait longer, but time is no longer our ally. Wouldst thou go with me to a place where thou canst be baptized by fellow Christiani?'

'Aye, I would.' I inhaled sharply the cool evening air. 'What else has been on thy mind?'

Lucius shifted his position on the bench. 'Many things. Some are still to be decided.' He was silent for a time. 'Enid— dost thou remember a few nights ago when I told thee that I loved thee?'

I laughed. 'Of course, Lucius! How could I ever forget that?'

He kissed my cheek. 'Dost thou love me then?'

I stared at him in the dusk. 'Lucius, I love thee dearly!'

I think he was smiling, but I could not tell for certain. 'My darling Enid, I know I can offer thee but little. I have no inheritance, nothing to call my own save the clothes on my back. I have no future in Rome as an illegitimate cripple of mixed blood. I cannot provide for thee as I ought. Any day, we might both be executed for our faith. But, despite all these things, dost thou love me enough to wed me and spend the rest of our lives—however long or short they may be—with one another?'

I gazed at him, my breath catching in my throat. Memories came rushing back: sunlight flooding the bare branches of the spring oaks, Telyn's shy smile as he said he wished to wed me, my young heart bursting with happiness…. Now there was darkness around us and uncertainty in the future, but the love that filled my soul was deeper, stronger, and more meaningful. I loved Lucius in a way I had never loved anyone else, not even Telyn, and I could never love another as I did him. 'Aye, Lucius,' I managed at last, breathlessly. 'Even if it meant certain death or the end of the world, I would wed thee.'

He put his hands on my cold cheeks and kissed my forehead. 'Come with me, then.' He rose, placing his crutch beneath his shoulder, and offered me his hand.

I took it, confused. The sun had set and no one was out on the streets but the guards, the farmers bringing in produce for tomorrow's market, and robbers. 'Are we to go now?'

'Aye, now. We have not a moment to lose.'

'Do Aurelia and Rufus know of this?'

'Nay, I have told no one—though Rufus knows of my intent. Come.' He led the way out of the atrium and into the chilly spring evening.

I shivered as an unexpected gust of wind pierced right through the thin stola I was wearing. Lucius halted, leaning on his crutch, and then drew me to himself, his left arm across my shoulders, wrapping his heavy military cloak around me. I sighed in contentment as he led the way through the darkened streets, his living warmth warding off the cold air.

Thunder rumbled in the distance and white lightning streaked across the city's horizon. A storm would break soon.

'Where are we going?' I whispered as we walked through streets which were quickly becoming unfamiliar to me.

He pulled the cloak tighter around my shoulders. 'Thou shalt see.'

CHAPTER XXIV

I KNEW NAUGHT of where we were going, only that the wind was beginning to rise, cold and fierce, bearing with it the sweet scent of rain. We were in one of the poorest districts of Rome, near the Tiber, and I could smell the stench some distance away—the filth of the one million persons who lived in the city, filth never washed away by the river. Yet I trusted Lucius and knew that whatever his purpose might be, it was reasonable.

He led me to a small shack among the warehouses and out-buildings near the docks and knocked on the door. Lightning flashed over the vast city, thunder rumbling to meet its cry, and raindrops began to fall from the dark and ominous sky.

A moment later, the door opened, revealing a dimly-lit room beyond. 'Who is it?' The voice was a man's, lacking the vibrancy of youth.

''Tis I, Lucius Justus Septimius, Brother Aquila.'

'Lucius, come in! Come in!' The man opened the door farther and gestured for us both to enter. Once safely inside, he shut the door against the rain and led us into a smaller room beyond.

The room was a simple one; a single oil lamp placed on the dirt floor provided light, a couple of straw pallets lay nearby, and a single dark doorway yawned into another room. A woman sat in the corner weaving. The simplicity reminded me of my home back in Britain, comfortable and familiar.

The man clapped Lucius on the back. 'Lucius, 'tis good to see thee after so long!'

Lucius was grinning, something I had not seen him do often. 'And thee, Aquila. It hath been long indeed.'

The woman rose, embracing Lucius as well, then looked at me. 'And who is this?' she asked kindly. Her smile and frank manner set me more at ease, though they were both strangers to me.

Lucius smiled at me sweetly, and warmth spread through my cold body at the look of fondness shining in his eyes. 'This is Enid, our new sister. She is of my own people.'

'Enid, thou art welcome among us. Please, sit down.' Aquila beckoned. 'So, what brings thee at this hour?' he questioned once we were both sitting comfortably on the floor.

'Thou hast heard of Julia's death?'

The eager smiles faded into sympathetic sadness, and I felt again the sharp pang of loss. Only yesterday and it seemed she was only waiting for us back home; except she was not, for she was no longer among us.

'Aye, I was there,' said Aquila gravely. His brown eyes were dark.

''Tis a tragic but beautiful thing to suffer for our Lord,' the woman added, her mellow voice deep with grief.

Lucius nodded slowly. 'Aquila, Priscilla, wouldst thou be willing to do something for me?'

'What may that be?' Aquila asked.

'Two things. Simple, maybe, but they would mean everything to Enid and I. Soon, we will no longer be in Rome—'

I looked up at him, confused, but he said nothing by way of explanation.

'—so I would wish these things to be done soon, and especially by thee.'

Aquila smiled, a twinkle in his eye. 'If thou tellest me what it is, I might acquiesce.'

'Wouldst thou baptize Enid?'

'And the second?'

'Wouldst thou marry us?'

'Should not thy cousin, Rufus, supply something formal for thy wedding?' Priscilla objected.

Lucius shook his head. 'I am not a Roman citizen due to my common-law birth. Enid has been freed from slavery with an informal manumission, so neither is she a citizen. 'Tis unnecessary to bring this matter to the courts.'

Aquila nodded. 'Aye, I will do it. 'Tis the least I can do for the grandson of Julia.' He rose to his feet and left the room.

I nudged Lucius gently and gave him a quizzical look.

He leaned over and whispered in my ear, his breath tickling my cheek, 'I will tell thee later.'

Aquila came back to us at that moment, carrying a small bowl of water. 'Would it be too much to ask for thee both to stand?' He handed the bowl to Priscilla and helped Lucius to his feet.

'Enid, art thou a servant of Christus?' Aquila questioned.

'I am,' I replied firmly, wondering at the same time with a cold sickness whether I would ever be asked these questions by a Roman who intended to put me to death should I answer aye.

'Dost thou believe in the One and only True God?'

'I do.' I did indeed, though few knew how difficult a path I had trodden to reach this belief.

'Dost thou believe that His Son, Jesus Christ, is the only hope for salvation and that there is no other way to be saved?'

'I do.'

'Then I baptize thee in the name of the Father, of His Son, and of the Holy Spirit.' Dipping his fingers in the water, Aquila placed his hand on my head, the cool, wet droplets running down my face.

I glanced at Lucius, who smiled encouragingly at me; I thought I saw tears in his eyes, though in the dim light I could not be certain. He was glad beyond words, even as I was, no matter how uncertain our near future might be.

'I thank thee,' I said to Aquila after he and Priscilla had embraced me as their fellow sister in Christ.

'Do not thank us. Thank our Father, Who has blessed us richly, above all that we could ever ask,' Priscilla answered, a beautiful smile on her aging face.

Aquila whispered something in Lucius' ear and then Lucius stood next to me, clasping my hand in his. Priscilla came to my other side, her gentle hand on my shoulder. Comforting warmth from both of them flowed into me, strengthening me in ways that words never could.

Aquila cleared his throat and looked at us both, the smile still in his eyes. 'Lucius, I hath known thee since thou wert first brought to the faith many years ago. Yet God hath known thee longer and hath set thee apart for His purposes and His glory; so also is it with Enid. I know that wherever He leads thee, there thou wilt both serve Him and glorify His name.

'Lucius, dost thou take Enid to be thy wife?'

'I do,' he replied without hesitation. His words falling upon my ears seemed to me the sweetest music ever written, and my lips parted in a joyful smile.

'Enid, dost thou take Lucius to be thy husband?'

'I do.' My words were scarcely more than a whisper; I could hardly believe my own happiness.

Lucius squeezed my hand gently and I looked up at him, a smile threatening to split my face, elation coursing through my veins. Tears of joy crinkled at the corners of my eyes, threatening to fall down my cheeks, but I no longer cared.

Aquila raised our joined hands, clasping them in his large, calloused ones. Then he lifted his eyes to heaven and prayed.

'Ah, Lord God! Thou knowest all things, from the rising of the sun to the scurrying of children in the streets of cities across the Roman Empire and the world. Thou knowest our hearts. Thou hast called us to be Thy children in this fallen world. Some Thou hast called to a life of singleness, but others to marriage. I pray now that Thou wouldst bless Lucius and Enid; bless their marriage, bless their service to Thee—whatever it may be—and if it be Thy will, bless them with many children. Guide them, direct their steps. May they be a witness to Thee unto the uttermost parts of the earth. Protect them from the Evil One and his wicked ways. May Thou be with us always, and may we always seek to glorify Thee. Thy will be done on earth as it is in heaven, from henceforth and forevermore. Amen.'

'Amen,' we echoed, a peaceful awe settling over me. Truly, the presence of God could be felt among us.

'Now go in peace, Lucius and Enid, and may God grant thee many joyful years together.' Aquila let go of our hands and he and his wife embraced us both warmly.

'Thou must be very careful when returning home,' Priscilla cautioned. 'Domitian's soldiers are everywhere.'

'I know, and I thank thee both,' Lucius said. 'I do not know if God will grant that we see each other again here on this earth, but one day we will meet again in paradise.'

We bade them farewell and went back into the rain- and windswept world.

The darkness was almost frightening to me after the lamplight of Aquila's house. I was still attempting to piece together all that had transpired. It felt like a dream, it had happened so quickly—but the cold water pouring from the skies could not be imagined.

Then Lucius embraced me tightly and I felt the cold no longer. '*Dw i'n caru chdi*, Enid,' he whispered in our native tongue, his voice and the words filling me with such emotion that I wanted to both sing and cry in one breath.

'*Dw i'n caru chdi, hefyd*, Lucius,' I whispered back, never wanting to let go.

He pressed his lips firmly against mine and warmth of another sort enveloped me, drowning me in passion.

'Lucius,' I said, after I had caught my breath. 'What didst thou mean, we will no longer be in Rome?'

'Come, we must return home soon before we are found out after curfew.' His arm was still across my shoulders, but we were walking now, returning the way we had come. 'As for that, I might as well tell thee now.'

'Does Rufus know?' I asked when he paused.

'He was the one who suggested it in the first place.'

'What is it?'

'Enid, wouldst thou like to go home?'

I drew my brows together in bewilderment at his strange question. 'We are.'

'Nay, I meant Britannia.'

I stopped walking, the world coming to a halt. My heart skipped a beat. 'What?' I gasped, not believing him.

'I meant what I said, Enid. Wouldst thou like to go home? Rome is no longer a safe place for us and besides, we never belonged. And I think thy people have not yet heard of our God.'

I stared at him. 'Truly? We are to return home—to our own land?'

He was about to answer me when we saw the night watch a few streets away and quickened our pace. We did not speak again until we were safely inside the dark atrium of the Septimius villa, the rain drumming on the roof.

All the servants had retired for the night, as had Aurelia and Rufus. I waited for Lucius to take off his cloak and lay it over a chair to dry before he took up his crutch again and joined me. 'Enid,' he spoke softly, 'dost thou still not believe me?'

'I can hardly believe any of this is real.' I slipped my arms around him.

He chuckled softly as he embraced me. 'Aye, I understand. 'Tis hard for me as well. But art thou willing to go with me to Britannia?'

'I am willing to follow thee anywhere, but especially to Britannia.'

'Art thou prepared to leave within three days?'

'Three days?' I exclaimed, pulling back and staring at him, though I could hardly see anything in the damp darkness.

'Aye, the ship that I have secured passage on for us both leaves within three days.'

I did not answer for some time, but leaned against him and felt his heart beat and his chest rise and fall with every breath.

'Aye,' I said at last, 'if I can say farewell to Agrippina, and Aurelia and Rufus.'

'I do not see why not,' Lucius stated. 'But I do have one thing more to ask thee.' Something in his tone struck me as mischievous.

'What might that be?' I asked cautiously.

'Sleep with me tonight—and every night,' he said ever so softly, his breath tickling my ear.

My face grew hot, my ears burning, though I longed for it as much as he did. 'Lucius, thou needest not ask me that. We are wedded now. I will be apart from thee no longer.'

'Come then, the night grows old.' With another kiss, he took my hand and together we left the atrium to the wet blackness of the Aprilis night.

I opened my eyes the next morning and was surprised to find Lucius fast asleep beside me, his black hair tousled and unruly. I blinked, remembering then what had taken place only a few hours ago, and I smiled in thankful joy.

I pulled the bedclothes up around my bare shoulders and closed my eyes, determined to enjoy every moment of this season of bliss while it lasted.

Three more days, and then all I knew would be changed forever.

CHAPTER XXV

THE MORNING AFTER Lucius and I were wedded, Aurelia and I went to her father's villa so I could bid Agrippina farewell. It was strange to return to that place, my feet treading the familiar streets for the last time, a bitter wave of nostalgia rising as I entered the door. Memories came flooding back—memories of the first time I had stood in that atrium with nothing but my name to call my own; memories of meeting Lucius, little knowing how my life would be changed forever; memories of leaving for Aurelia's new home and my new life. And now I would never see it again.

'Why, Aurelia, what a surprise!' Honoria embraced her daughter as we entered. 'I did not expect to see thee for several more days. What brings thee here? Is Rufus in good health?'

'Aye, he is in good health. His avia died a few days past, so I thought to visit thee and give him some time by himself.' Aurelia smiled sweetly.

I noted that she did not specify how Julia had died, and I approved of her discretion. The less others knew about it, the better. I nodded towards Aurelia and went down to the kitchen. I wanted to take my time in saying goodbye to Agrippina and not be rushed.

'Marcella!' Agrippina greeted me with a smile. ''Tis a welcome sight to see thee again so soon.'

The other slaves left the culina to take up their duties elsewhere, leaving the two of us alone. Bread was baking in the oven, and the smell made my mouth water. Tears gathered at the corners of my eyes and I blinked them back with difficulty. I knew this place so well and soon I would see it no more.

'I am to leave for my homeland, Agrippina. I have been given my freedom.'

The cook stared at me. 'Mistress Aurelia has given thee thy freedom?'

'Aye. It happened yesterday.'

'But why? And who will serve her in thy place?'

'When I was ill, another slave tended her, so she is used to someone else now. Besides, some things happened that led to great changes in the household.' My wording was hesitant and awkward. How much was too much to tell? 'Aurelia and Rufus thought it best they grant me my freedom. And Aurelia says that I have served her long enough and have most certainly earned it.'

'Well, I shall be sorry to see thee go forever. Wilt thou not stay? Rufus and Aurelia will let thee stay with them, will they not?' She smacked her floured hands clean on her apron and took it off, gesturing for me to sit on the stool across from hers.

'Rufus and Aurelia have been kind in giving me a place with them, aye, but while I do appreciate their kindness, 'tis time I returned home. Besides, my husband wishes me to go to Britannia with him since it is his own home also,' I ventured, no longer trying to keep a smile off my face.

'Thy husband? Why, Marcella! Since when...' Her voice trailed off in amazement, the grey sunlight reflecting off the floor onto her face.

I smiled. 'Lucius. Dost thou remember him?'

'That British youth who was friends with Augustus?'

I nodded, a pleasant blush spreading across my features. My face almost hurt from smiling so broadly. Yet I could not help but smile; I was still overwhelmed by happiness and could hardly believe this was not all some wonderful dream soon to be shattered.

'Well, I do not know him beyond hearing *of* him, but any-one who can bring such a smile to thy face must be very special indeed. Art thou happy now, Marcella?'

'Aye, I am very happy.' My words were scarcely louder than a whisper and I glanced down at my clasped hands, blissful memories of the evening before rushing to mind.

Agrippina smiled. 'It took thee five years, but thou hast found happiness in the end.' Her voice hitched in her throat. 'I am glad for thee. And I wish thee well in Britannia, truly. But I shall miss thee dearly.' Her eyes began to water.

The smile vanished from my face. I longed to tell her the best reason for my happiness, but 'twas too dangerous. Not only for myself and Lucius, but also for Aurelia and Rufus, and I did not wish to cause them harm. 'Agrippina, I shall miss thee dearly as well. I have not forgotten thy kindness to me these past few years. I owe much to thee and I thank thee.' I took her rough, calloused hand in mine and stroked it gently.

'Marcella! Art thou ready to leave?' Aurelia's voice came down the stairs from above.

'I must go.' I rose to my feet reluctantly.

'Marcella, wait.' Agrippina took a step forward and embraced me tightly. I wrapped my arms around her also, feeling her frame shudder slightly.

When she pulled back, she was brushing away tears. 'I wish thee well, Marcella. I will not forget thee,' she said with a sad smile.

I smiled in return, a heaviness in my chest.

Farewell. What a sorrowful word. It meant goodbye and finality and losing what once was without any chance or hope of ever returning back. The poets were right; there was no way back through the waters of Lethe.

As I left the Aurelian villa for the last time, I looked back over my shoulder to watch it disappear in the distance, the sunlight striking the familiar white marble walls and nearly blinding my eyes.

I would never see it again.

Aurelia and Rufus were the only ones who accompanied Lucius and me to the docks that misty morning in late spring as the rising sun tinted the wraith-like swaths of fog on the water a rosy gold. The air was still, but already it was warm.

They bade us a tearful farewell on the docks. Lucius and Rufus spoke to each other, but I did not hear what they said. Aurelia embraced me tightly and kissed me on both cheeks, tears streaming freely down both our faces. I was saying goodbye to the world I had known for five years and the people I had grown to love in my own rough way. Though I had once hated them, I would now miss them dearly.

We boarded the ship that would take us home, waving goodbye to the couple still standing on the quay. The rowers below us rolled out their oars and the rhythmic beatings of the hortator began to sound as dawn broke over the world. The shoreline of Rome's harbor vanished into the eastern horizon while I faced the sunrise with Lucius by my side.

''Tis hard to believe, is it not?' he asked me softly.

'To believe what?'

'That after so long we are going home.' He looked down at me and smiled, the sunlight sparkling in his green-gold eyes.

I smiled back and leaned my head against his shoulder. Indeed, I could scarcely believe that in a few weeks I would land on familiar shores and return to my own people. If the Iceni would not receive Lucius because of his Roman ancestry, there was always another valley in which to make our dwelling. But I did not think my people would be so distrusting of him—of us both.

'Going home,' I repeated. 'It sounds strange, perhaps because…' My voice trailed away into the salty air of the Mediterranean.

'Because?'

'I never imagined I would ever return to Britannia, let alone'—I glanced up at him—'with thee.'

He bent and kissed my forehead. 'I know. Last time I returned to these shores, I thought the same. It felt odd returning to the land I had known so well as a child, and yet everything was different from what I remembered and expected…I hope 'tis not too different for thee.' His dark brows drew together in concern.

I stood on tiptoes and planted a kiss on his cheek. 'With thee by my side, I do not fear what may come.'

The creaking timbers of the gently-rocking ship snapped me from my musings and I blinked, my blurred vision focusing at last on the swaying lantern that cast dancing shadows on the walls and floor. A week or more had passed, and the reality had yet to fully sink into my heart. It still felt like a dream—a pleasant dream, but a dream nonetheless.

I had dwelt in Rome as a slave and later as a freed woman for around five years. For those first few years, I had hated every moment away from those I loved with no hope of ever going back. I had always wished to return to my homeland, wished for my freedom, but I never expected it to really happen—let alone in the way it did.

I rose and went to the writing desk that hung out from the wall, pulled up a stool, and sat down. The events of the past five years flashed before my eyes, each memory lingering for a moment before making way for the next—fragments of the life that had been, the life of which I had spoken but little, and never in full detail.

I reached down into the satchel at my feet and withdrew several thin, double-sided wax tablets and a sharpened stylus. I tapped the stylus against my lips, trying to make sense out of it all and put it in a logical sequence.

At last I pressed the pen into the soft wax, creating the characters that formed the letters, words, and phrases that told my tale. For everyone has a story to tell; this one was my own.

My father had always warned me of the Redcrests. Instruments of evil—thus he named them. But it was not until that day that I understood why.

They destroyed everything: my life, my hopes, and my dreams. They forced their ruthless way into my life and left me shattered in the dust with no more worth than forgotten shards of clay. They say slaves are weak and ignorant. But I proved them wrong. I vowed that day that I would never love them. That I would not speak unless spoken to. That I would treat them with the same cold cruelty and indifference they had dealt me. I turned my broken trust into icy stone and locked my true self away, buried beneath dullness and feigned stupidity, thinking it would so remain until I died.

Yet it was I who was in the wrong. Lucius melted the ice and showed me there was still good in the world. Not all men are evil. In some still lies a pure heart of humility and respect, if only thou knowest how to look for it.

Love was still to be had, promise-keepers still existed, hope still remained in the mortal world. But neither of us knew how high the cost would be....

I paused and looked up through the open porthole, soaking in the brilliance of the blue sky against the darker sapphire of the sea. The wind bore the bittersweet scent of salt, and I inhaled it deeply before continuing.

...The harpist's hands danced across the silver strings, shimmering in the flamelight, the music rising to the roof and falling like shimmering rain upon the hearers. The smoking torches thrust back the darkness of twilight and the smell of burning peat hung in the chieftain's hall as all waited in expectation for the bard to sing. Then he began, his mellow voice rising and falling in cadencing rhythm with

his hands, uttering forth the words of the well-known tale into the respectful silence—

'Enid!'

I jumped, my stylus making a deep gouge in the wax.

'Oh, Enid!' Lucius laughed. 'I did not mean to frighten thee.'

I turned to him and smiled. 'No harm done. What is it?' I rose to my feet, laying aside the tablets. My story would take a long time in the recording, and I did not wish to tire myself out too soon.

'Come with me out onto the deck. We are nearing the shore of Britannia.'

My throat tightened. *Britannia. We are almost there.* 'Aye, I will come,' I said, giving him my shoulder to lean on instead of his crutch.

Out on deck, one could hear more clearly the rhythmic splashing of the oars below, even though there was a strong wind helping with the sails. A blinding sun shone down from a cloudless sky and I could feel it heating my bare head, glistening off the crimson strands of hair that I wore unbound.

Together, Lucius and I made our way to the railing, looking ahead at the horizon soon to darken at any moment. The wind was cold and tossed my hair unmercifully, making Lucius laugh again.

I was glad to hear him laugh; he did it so seldom, and even less often since Julia's death. But he was laughing now, and I reveled in the sound, feeling warm, safe, and content.

His strong arm lay across my shoulders and I leaned my forehead against his neck, closing my eyes. I never dreamed that such happiness could ever be mine. Even when I had surrendered and given all that was me unto the God of the Christiani, I never thought such joy could be possible to obtain.

'Land ho!' The cry of the lookout high in the crow's nest thundered down to us and I opened my eyes, squinting hard against the brightness of day.

There on the northwest horizon rose the dark green and misty hills of my homeland.

'Dost thou see it, Enid?' Lucius whispered into my ear.

'Aye, I see it.' My voice was quiet and awed as the beautiful reality of it sank in and overwhelmed me. 'God has been so good to me.'

'He has been very good to us both.' Lucius wrapped both of his arms about me and kissed me gently.

I smiled and looked out again as the shores of Britannia drew ever nearer, and with them our new life together.

I was no longer a captive to the dark imprisonment of sin, rejecting the light. I was no longer fighting against my new life of slavery and my broken past of freedom. I was no longer at a loss as how to survive as a freed slave, belonging to neither the Roman nor British world. The struggle was over, the battle was won.

I was no longer caught between two worlds.

I was home.

GLOSSARY

Agrippina *(Ah-grih-pee-na)* – fictional Greek cook in the Aurelian household

Aprilis *(Ae-pril-lis)* – the 4th month in the Roman calendar

Atrium *(Ae-tree-um)* – central room of a Roman house; equivalent to our modern-day living room

Aurelia *(Ae-rill-leah)* – fictional mistress and friend of Enid

Aurelius Augustus Trajan *(Aer-rill-lee-is Uh-gust-is Tray-jan)* – the fictional senator and father of Aurelia

Augustus Aurelius Trajan *(Uh-gust-is Aer-rill-lee-is Tray-jan)* – the fictional brother of Aurelia

Auxiliary *(Auhx-ill-ler-ee)* – volunteer legionaries who were not Roman citizens by birth

Avia *(Ah-vee-ah)* – Latin for 'grandmother'

Boudicca *(Bow-dish-ah)* – British chieftainess who raised a failed rebellion against Rome around 60-61 A.D.

Brenyn *(Bren-nin)* – fictional daughter of Boudicca

Brynmor *(Brin-more)* – fictional brother of Enid

Bulla *(Bull-lah)* – a type of necklace with a pouch that contained charms, worn by ancient Roman children as a type of protection from evil spirits

Caligo sanguis *(Cah-lig-oh sang-oo-is)* – Latin for 'blood mist'

Caradoc *(Care-ah-doc)* – fictional harper in Enid's village

Castrum *(Cast-trum)* – plot of land used as a military camp

Cena *(Sen-nah)* – Latin for 'dinner'

Centurion *(Sen-ter-ee-un)* – a commander of a group of around one hundred legionaries. Senior centurions commanded cohorts or took senior staff roles in their legion. Centurions were also found in the Roman navy

Chaplet *(Chap-let)* – a garland or wreath worn on a person's head

Christiani *(Chrish-tee-an-ee)* – Latin insult for 'followers of the Way' or 'followers of Christ'; from it comes our modern word, 'Christian'

Christus *(Chrees-tus)* – Latin for 'Christ'; means 'chosen one' or 'Messiah'

Culina/Culinae *(Cuh-leen-ah/ae)* – Roman kitchen(s)

Dewch yma *(Deh-o-ch [guttural ch sound like the gh in ugh] yih-ma)* – Welsh (a Celtic tongue in the Brythonic family of languages) for 'come here'

Dennis *(Den-nis)* – fictional steward in the Aurelian household

Dos *(Dawhs)* – Roman word for dowry

Durovernum Cantiacorum *(Dero-ver-num Kant-ee-ah-core-um)* – a town and hillfort in Roman Britain (modern-day Canterbury in Kent)

Dw i'n caru chdi/dw i'n caru chdi, hefyd *(Doo een car-ee ch-[wet* gh *sound as in* ugh*]-dee heh-vid)* – Welsh phrase meaning 'I love you' or 'I love you too'

Enid *(Ee-nid)* – fictional British slave girl

Esquiline Hill *(Es-quill-line Hill)* – one of seven hills in the city of Rome; was the location of the villas of Rome's wealthier citizens

Februaris *(Feb-rue-air-is)* – the 12th month in the Roman calendar

Ffionn *(Fee-on)* – fictional brother of Enid

Filias *(Fill-ee-as)* – Latin for 'girls'

Flammeum *(Flah-may-oom)* – Roman bridal veil, named for its flame colour

Fy nghariad *(Vee nn-har-ee-ad)* – Welsh for 'my sweetheart'

Gaius Suetonius Paulinus *(Guy-is Sue-tone-ee-is Paul-lin-is)* – a Roman general and governor of Britannia, best known as the commander who defeated the rebellion of Boudicca

Gratias tibi *(Grah-tee-as tee-bee)* – Latin for 'thank you'

Gwyn ap Nudd *(Gwin app Nudth)* – king of the fae folk and ruler of the underworld in Welsh mythology, said to roam the skies at night with his wild pack of demons known as the Wild Hunt

Honoria *(On-nor-ree-ah)* – the fictional wife of Aurelius

Hypogeum *(High-podge-ee-um)* – the name for the area beneath the Colosseum

Ilar *(Ill-ar)* – fictional brother of Enid

Intrabit *(Inn-trah-bit)* – Latin for 'enter'

Ioan *(Yo-in)* – fictional father of Enid and chieftain of the village

Ita *(Ee-tah)* – Latin for 'yes'

Julia Laelia Maxima *(Jew-lee-ah Lay-lee-ah Max-ih-mah)* – fictional sister of Gaius Suetonius Paulinus

Justus Julius Septimius *(Just-is Jew-lee-is Sept-tih-mee-is)* – fictional nephew of Gaius Suetonius Paulinus

Lares *(Lar-is)* – a Roman guardian deity that protected the Roman household

Legatus *(Leg-gate-is)* – the highest ranking officer in a Roman legion

Legio IX Hispana *(Ledge-ee-oh Hiss-pan-nah)* – the Ninth Iberian Legion

Legionary *(Liege-on-air-ee)* – a professional heavy infantryman of the Roman army

Lucius Justus Septimius *(Loo-shee-is Just-is Sept-tih-mee-is)* – fictional son of Justus

Mabon *(Mah-bon)* – mid-harvest festival from Welsh mythology

Marcella *(Mar-sell-ah)* – Enid's slavehood name

Martius *(Marsh-ee-us)* – the 1st month of the Roman calendar

Mater *(Mah-ter)* – Latin for 'mother'

Mea *(May-ah)* – Latin for 'my' (feminine form)

Milites Medici *(Mill-ih-tis Meh-dee-see)* – Roman military doctor

Mulsum *(Mull-sum)* – a popular wine and honey mixture

Nepos *(Nay-poss)* – Latin for 'grandson'

Pater *(Pah-ter)* – Latin for 'father'

Peristylium *(Pear-is-stye-lee-um)* – private Roman garden

Populi *(Pop-you-lee)* – Latin for 'people'

Quaestor *(Kay-stor)* – a public official in Ancient Rome

Quintus Petillius Cerialis *(Quin-tis Pet-till-lee-is Kare-ee-ah-lis)* – a Roman general and administrator who served in Britain during Boudicca's rebellion; he was the legate of Legio IX Hispania

Rufus Quintus Septimius *(Roo-fis Kwin-tis Sept-i-mee-is)* – fictional grandson of Julia and cousin of Lucius

Servii *(Sair-vee)* – the class of slaves

Sesterces *(Ses-ter-seas)* – Roman coin worth about $2; plural form is sestertii

Solea *(Sole-ee-ah)* – sandals worn only in the house

Stola *(Stole-ah)* – similar to the toga, it was worn by women. Above the girdle, upwards it was open at the sides and fastened at the shoulders. It was worn over the tunic, which made the main dress of everyone in the Roman Empire

Tablinum *(Tab-lin-um)* – the office of the man of the house

Telyn *(Tay-lin)* – fictional sweetheart of Enid

Tullia *(Tool-lee-ah)* – fictional cook in the Septimius household

Toga praetexta *(Toh-gah prey-text-tah)* – a tunic bordered by purple; worn by the children of upper classes until youths reached manhood and girls were married off

Valdete *(Val-det-ae)* – Latin form of farewell

Venta Icenorum *(Vent-tah Ice-sen-nor-um)* – a Roman fort-town in the area of the tribal Iceni; now modern-day Caistor St. Edmund in Norfolk, England

Vexillatio *(Vex-ill-ah-tee-oh)* – a detachment of a Roman legion formed as a temporary task force created by the Roman army of the Principate. It was named from the standard carried by legionary detachments, the *vexillum* (plural *vexilla*), which bore the emblem and name of the parent legio

ACKNOWLEDGMENTS

Writing is often a lonely task.

It involves hours of sitting and using nothing but your brain and every ounce of creativity and energy you have—not to mention stashes of tea and chocolate and occasionally tears. But on the sidelines, I have been privileged to have some of the most amazing people cheer me on and to them I owe the world. This story would not be the same without you.

To my Lord and Savior, Who inspired this story in the very beginning, and Who has been with me all the way through. Thank You for letting me tell this tale.

I would also like to thank my dearest friend, Rebekah Hou, for telling me this story should be written. I probably would never have written it otherwise.

Thirdly, I want to give a shout-out to WattPairsMentorship for hosting the mentorship program and to M. Dalto for helping me make this book better through various edits and polishing. Thanks to my fellow mentors and mentees for giving me the encouragement I needed to reach the end: Gladys Quinn, Taryn, Xandria, Cassidy, Marianna Hubrism, and Amy Gillespie. And to Sevannah Storm and Jasmine Shouse for your immense help during the querying process.

My eternal thanks belong to my beta-readers: Celia Cahill, Lucy Kennedy, and to my dearest friend and schiva, Brianna De Man, for helping me make this story the book I envisioned. To Verity Buchanan, for always being so supportive and helping me fix the blurb and letting me come to you with my endless questions whether the wording of something was right. And of course, to my amazing editor Elisabeth Hayse who made this story even stronger, and Deborah O'Carroll, my copy-editor, for catching the small mistakes I had left.

To my friend and talented graphic designer, Faera Lane, for capturing my vision in the lovely cover she made.

To "Cross" and Wim and Mercy Buchanan and everyone else who voted for me like mad in The Fiction Awards 2019 on Wattpad. To win a popularity award on that website with a book so controversial is an achievement that wouldn't have been possible without you.

To Stephen Howard and Lydia Hayse and the team at New Degree Press for being willing to step in last-minute and help me put together everything needed for my promotional video. The final result awed me.

To my launch team for being the most amazing people who listen to my odd rants about new things I am discovering with this story, who move me to tears with your posts on social media and seeing you get excited for a book you've never read, and who have supported this novel's publication.

This book also owes its published form to the following people who preordered this book and have supported me in many ways. Some of you are family, some are friends, some are strangers who thought my book was worth investing in, some are fellow writers and musicians that I've had the privilege to get to know over the last several years. I cannot thank you enough for supporting me and my book:

Deborah O'Carroll

Alyona Hill

Victoria Nicol

Hannah Yu

Rebekah Hou

Verity Buchanan

Jennifer McKeithen

Randall Beecham

Brianna De Man

Kayla Miller

Jasmine Shouse

Fallon Davis

Breanna Marsh

Rachel Johnson

Sarah Penney

Lincoln Naylor

Gabrielle Paul

Byron Weigler

Evangeline Mount

Titus Alexander

Stephanie Smith

Elizabeth Russell

Rae Graham

Hannah Ward

Mary Sivils

Eric Koester

Jim Menefee

Mercy Buchanan

Sally Benjamin

Robert C. Noble

Jennifer Peterson

Bailey Gaines

Stacie Eirich

Jeanne Nicol

Alex Nova

Ethan Wennerstrom

Aria Maher

Priya Petty

Bonnie J. Bodo

Elizabeth Reiss

Morgan Matich

Caitlyn Wetzel

Melissa Little

MC van Delft

Amy Gillespie

Brittni E. Anderson

N.C. Kay

Alisha Sheaffer

Victoria Smith

Julianne Bieron

Stephanie Bird
Maria Clarissa Shanisha
Julianne Arambula
Savannah Cooper
Ryan Ouellette
Janice Verhoog
Stephen Howard

David Fisher
Cody Goff
Aria Miller
Joseph Conkle
Amanda McCrina
Regina Appleby

Lastly, to my "gang" who not only inspired some of the characters in this story, but have also been some of the most encouraging people I know. To Frankie Vitale who inspired Ffionn and Rufus, and his brother Luca who inspired the name and appearance of Lucius. To Isaac (Ilar) Willour, my "adopted" brother, for somehow having faith that I could write and publish this book; to Corina Peppo, for your sweet friendship and prayers during the stressful mentorship; to Ike Graham, for that text you sent me, telling me not to give up and that I would finish in spite of everything—I will never forget it; and to Brayden (Brynmor) Peppo, for your friendship and support—and in answer to that question you asked me once if it all was worth it, I can say now that yes, it was.

And thank you, from the bottom of my heart, to the readers whose names I do not know and probably will never meet, for being a part of this journey.

You all have made it worthwhile.

ABOUT THE AUTHOR

Cheyenne van Langevelde is a young author and musician whose greatest passion is weaving tales through story and song. When not struggling to attempt the most metaphorical prose, she enjoys composing and recording soundtrack pieces for books, practicing calligraphy and Irish dance, and studying the Welsh language. She occasionally emerges into the real world to restock her chocolate supply, which she hoards like a dragon would his gold. *Between Two Worlds* is her debut novel.

You can follow her on her website and social sites listed below:

Website: https://www.thedancingbardess.com
Instagram: @thedancingbardess
Twitter: @dancing_bardess
Goodreads: Cheyenne van Langevelde